Betsy's Wedding

Betsy's Wedding

MAUD HART LOVELACE

Illustrated by Vera Neville

HarperTrophy
A Division of HarperCollinsPublishers

ACKNOWLEDGMENTS

The verse on page 143 was written by Darragh Aldrich and appeared in the *Minneapolis Tribune* in 1914. The verse on page 248 is adapted from a verse by Earle Buell which appeared in the *Minneapolis Tribune* in 1917. The epigraph is from "For Katrina's Sun Dial" by Henry Van Dyke, and the lines on page 2 are from "America for Me" by Henry Van Dyke; both from *The Poems of Henry Van Dyke*, copyright 1911, 1939 by Charles Scribner's Sons, New York. The lines from "Silk o' the Kine" by Alfred Noyes, which appear on page 75, are from *Poems*, copyright 1906, 1934 by Alfred Noyes, reprinted by permission of J. B. Lippincott Company, Philadelphia, and A. P. Watt and Sons, London.

For

LILLIAN HAMMONS WAKEFIELD

Contents

Hours fly,
Flowers die.
New days,
New ways,
Pass by.
  Love stays.
    —Henry Van Dyke

1

HOME AGAIN

Almost choked with excitement and joy, Betsy Ray
leaned against the railing as the *S.S. Richmond* sailed
serenely into New York City's inner harbor. The morning was misty, and since they had passed through the
Narrows, she had seen only sky and water—and a gull,
now and then—as though they were still out in the
Atlantic. But she knew she had come home.

> *... home again, and home again, America for*
> *me!*
> *My heart is turning home again, and there I*
> *long to be ...*

Betsy chanted softly to herself. She gripped the rail hard.

And Joe's waiting for me! she thought. Oh, I hope he's going to like me as well as he used to! I hope I look nice.

It wasn't her fault if she didn't. She had beautified herself as thoroughly as possible, but that wasn't much, for she shared a stateroom with three older women—and had been lucky to have one at all. The outbreak of war in Europe had crowded to overflowing all American-bound ships. On the *Richmond* many men had slept on deck. There had been three sittings at table—the dishes were barely washed between—while talk went on and on about the adventures, the mishaps, the dangers the passengers had encountered in getting out of Germany, or France, or England. Talk was the only diversion for the vessel had sailed its fearful way in darkness.

It had been a contrast to the gay trip on the *Columbic* which had taken Betsy abroad in January. This was September, 1914. She was twenty-two years old.

I'm glad of my new Paris suit, she thought. The suit, of dark blue wool, was flattering to her slender figure. The skirt was long; the jacket belted with crushed crimson satin. A dark hat framed her shining face. Not just her eyes were shining. Something inside was shining because she was meeting Joe.

Joe Willard had been important to Betsy since high school days in Deep Valley, Minnesota. He had not gone with her Crowd—by his own choice, for his good looks, humor, and warmth drew people to him. But he was an orphan with scant pocket money and no time to waste. He had worked after school on the *Deep Valley Sun*.

He had worked on the *Minneapolis Tribune* during the following two years when he and Betsy attended the University of Minnesota. They had considered themselves almost engaged. But then Joe had won a scholarship to Harvard. He had gone East, getting work on the *Boston Transcript*—for Joe was always working. And they had quarreled.

"It was my fault," Betsy said to the gulls, swooping past her toward the foam that boiled up along the vessel's side. "Flirting with someone I didn't give a hang for! No wonder Joe stopped writing!"

She had felt very badly about it but she had been too stubborn to try to make up.

When her trip abroad was planned—because she wanted to be a writer, and her father had thought she would profit from foreign travel—Betsy had not even let Joe know that she was sailing from the port of Boston. As it happened, however, she had caught a glimpse of him there.

He had been one of a group of reporters interviewing

3

Mrs. Main-Whittaker, the author, and Betsy had recognized his walk. Joe Willard met life with a challenge which showed in his swinging walk. His blond hair had looked the same too, brushed back in a pompadour. The close-cropped mustache had been new. But Betsy had known him, and the sight of him had brought all her heartache flooding back.

She had sailed away determined to forget Joe Willard but she had not forgotten him, during her journey into the Great World.

"I didn't forget him and I didn't stop loving him," she said. She spoke softly for there were people at her elbows now. The sun had come out, and the bay which had been gray was greenish-blue, full of dancing whitecaps. Suddenly a murmur ran along the railing, rising to glad cries and long-drawn-out "Ahs!" of admiration and wonder. Through a crack in the misty clouds ahead, the towers of Manhattan had come into view.

They looked unreal, white and glistening among the clouds, like the towers of a city in a fairy book—or the holy city in the Book of Revelation, Betsy thought, gazing.

"Why, it's Lilliput! You feel you could take it up on the palm of your hand!" a man near her exclaimed.

As the ship churned forward, the buildings grew more substantial, but still they were only white pencils standing on end. It did not seem possible that these could be powerful masses of steel and concrete and stone, the celebrated skyscrapers of New York.

"There's the Woolworth Building!" someone shouted, and everyone stared at that world-famous pile, the highest one of all.

New Yorkers all around her were eagerly identifying other famous buildings, but these cries died down. Gleaming in sunlight, majestic, benign, the Goddess of Liberty had come into view.

That figure with the upflung arm caused silence to fall along the line of travelers returning to their peaceful homeland from a Europe blazing with war. France, Betsy remembered, had given the United States this statue in tribute to the American fight for freedom. And now France was fighting for her freedom!

Tears blurred Betsy's eyes but they weren't just for France. They were for America, and Joe, and because she was so glad to be back. She cried and cried, wiping away the tears with both her hands, so she could look ahead.

Now everyone was shouting frantically again, above the din of whistles and hollow-sounding horns. They were exclaiming that a phantom bridge at their right was the wonderful Brooklyn Bridge. They were pointing out Ellis Island where immigrants stopped before entering the United States.

There were ferries, ploughing placidly between Staten Island and the Battery, and more ocean-going steamships, and grimy freighters, and busy little tugs. There was even a delicate four-masted schooner, speaking in silence of a gentle past.

Joe would like that schooner, Betsy thought, as she had thought so often when seeing lovely things during her travels. And then it came to her that in a few moments she could tell him about it, about anything she cared to, and she started crying again.

They had turned up the Hudson—it seemed to be called the North River—and the waterfront was lined with ships, flying flags of many nations. A pair of tugs began to nudge the *Richmond* into one of the rows of jutting piers. The water was quieter here although it still smelled salt and fishy. All mists had gone, and the sky above the waiting city was lavender blue, full of light spirals of cloud.

Betsy looked at the barnlike structure rising at the end of the pier. Joe was in there!

And I must look like an absolute fright! she thought, wiping her eyes with new determination. She took a powder puff out of the handbag swinging from her arm and powdered her hot cheeks. She found a tiny bottle and touched her earlobes with a new Parisian scent.

Joe would be waiting, strangely enough, because she had met Mrs. Main-Whittaker in Paris. Betsy had been too stubborn to write and make up their quarrel until that famous lady had inadvertently shown her a way. Mrs. Main-Whittaker had praised the story of her departure from Boston which Joe had written for the *Transcript*, and that had given Betsy the excuse her pride needed. She had passed along the compliment in a carefully casual note.

To be sure, she forgot in her confusion to include any address. But she had told him that she was bound for London and had mentioned chattily something Mrs. Main-Whittaker had said: that Betsy, because she liked to write stories, should be sure to read the column of Personals—the Agony Column, it was called—in the *London Times*.

That had been enough for Joe, who always knew how to find a way. After the Germans marched into Belgium he had cabled to the Agony Column.

> *Betsy. The Great War is on but I hope ours is over. Please come home. Joe.*

And Betsy had cabled in reply:

> *Joe. Please meet S.S. Richmond arriving New York September 7. Love. Betsy.*

She had been bold, she thought now, color flooding up into her cheeks, to put in that "love." And she had been assuming a good deal when she asked him to meet her in New York. He had been graduated in June, but she felt sure he was continuing on the *Transcript* in Boston.

A girl named Victoria came up and tugged at Betsy's arm. "Have you remembered everything?"

"Everything. Even the doll for Tacy's baby." Betsy's smile which showed white teeth parted a little in front was friendly like Betsy herself. Victoria knew all about

7

Tacy, Betsy's best friend, who was expecting a baby which Betsy was expecting to be a girl.

The doll, bought in Germany, was a bulky package piled, with Betsy's suitcases and steamer trunk, out in the passageway. Her umbrella and camera were on the steamer chair behind her. She picked them up, for the liner was bumping now, conclusively, against the pier.

Betsy and Victoria were caught up in the crowd pushing toward the gangplank. Betsy went with deliberate slowness for her heart was thumping. She was even trembling a little. And she mustn't, she told herself, act excited. Joe would expect her to be poised and dignified after almost a year in Europe.

She and Tacy had joked in their letters about Betsy's acquiring "an indefinable Paris air."

"But it's no joke! That's just what I ought to have," Betsy declared firmly. She adjusted her hat to its most effective slant and patted her curls—she hoped they were still curls, but the sea air didn't agree with Betsy's hair. She remembered the models she had seen parading at Longchamps. They had that fashionable, spineless look called "the debutante slouch." Betsy let herself slink into it now.

Victoria understood.

"No need to get fixed for him yet," she said. "We have to go through Customs, you know. People aren't allowed to come in without passes, and with the war on, they'll be hard to get."

But Joe, Betsy knew, was the kind to get a pass no matter how strict regulations might be, and she continued to saunter like a Longchamps model down the gangplank and into the barnlike warehouse. This was divided into sections with the letters of the alphabet posted above to indicate where the passengers might find their luggage and open it for waiting Customs officials. Bidding Victoria an affectionate good-by, Betsy sauntered toward the "R's."

But suddenly she stood up straighter than an arrow. Not standing under the "R's," but swinging toward her with a cane hung over his arm, came a stocky blond young man.

Betsy ran toward him.

The next thing she knew he had his arms around her. She had dropped her umbrella and her new hat was knocked off but she didn't care. He was holding her close and saying over and over, "Oh, Betsy! Betsy!" And Betsy, when she could lift her tear-wet face from where it was crushed into his woolly shoulder, tried to say "Joe! Joe!" but she couldn't because he was kissing her and she was kissing him.

Joe held her off at arm's length. Under his blond pompadour and tufted golden brows, his eyes were blazingly bright. Blushing, Betsy rescued her hat, and Joe picked up her umbrella.

He took hold of her arm in a strong and purposeful grasp.

"Let's get this Customs business out of the way quick," he said. "And then we'll go to Tiffany's and get you a ring. And then—" he turned swiftly to look into her face—"when can we get married?"

2
JOE'S PLAN

"But we have to be engaged a little while!" Betsy was explaining, an hour or so later, in front of the Pennsylvania Station.

Her trunk, her suitcases, and Tacy's doll had been checked and she had picked up her tickets. Mr. Ray had written Joe, asking him to make her reservations, and he had—on the latest train leaving New York that night which would make connections for Minneapolis in Chicago the following evening.

Betsy had given Joe his present, a British edition of Kipling's *Soldier Stories*. He had been pleased, but he had teased her about the Ray custom of bringing home presents. He and Betsy had met first in Joe's uncle's store in Butternut Center when she was buying home-presents after a visit to a farm.

"You Rays!" he scoffed. "Do you have a parchment scroll for recording these old family customs? Bringing home presents! Muffins for special occasions! Sunday night lunches!"

He stopped with a wide grin.

"That reminds me! Marriage is a fine old family custom. When are we going to get married?"

It was then Betsy had protested that they had to be engaged a little while.

A taxicab slued to a stop. "The Waldorf, skipper!" Joe said.

"The Waldorf!" Betsy's face was as bright as the corsage bouquet Joe had bought for her shoulder. She had heard all her life of the famous Waldorf-Astoria Hotel. They rolled in a great tide of motor cars and carriages to the corner of Fifth Avenue and Thirty-fourth Street, and Joe helped her out, her green taffeta petticoat swishing.

Inside the celebrated door, she was pleased to remember that her suit came from Paris, for the women strolling along the marble corridor known as Peacock Alley were extremely modish.

But I have the handsomest escort! Betsy thought. He was so poised, too, amid this sophisticated splendor. She walked proudly with his hand gripping her arm, and gazed up at the carved and frescoed ceiling and around at deep leather chairs, rich oriental rugs.

At the Rose Room door Joe checked his hat and cane. The violins seemed to be singing just for them. They were seated at a window table, and a deferential waiter spread Betsy's jacket over the back of her chair, and she transferred Joe's flowers to her blouse—snowy crêpe de Chine with pleated frills at neck and wrists.

While Joe ordered, she looked out at Fifth Avenue—or tried to. The broad windows held a procession of curious faces as passersby paused to look in.

"They look in to see the celebrities," Joe explained. "Celebrities like—oh, Betsy Ray! Author of 'Emma Middleton Cuts Cross Country.'"

"Joe, did you read that?"

"After your letter came, I hunted up an *Ainslee's*. Betsy!" His tone changed. "That was the happiest moment of my life—when your letter came."

"Was it?" Betsy asked tremulously.

"But now—this one is."

"It is for me, too."

Joe leaned closer, his blue eyes bright. "Today," he said, "I could do anything. I could swim seas, or topple mountains, or link the poles by tunnel. And that's why I believe I can persuade you to marry me soon."

Her cheeks turned to flames.

"Betsy," he said, "when your father wrote me, I thought at first that I wouldn't get those tickets. I thought, 'Why don't Betsy and I just get married and go to Boston?'"

"Joe!"

"I know. But I thought again. A Ray ought to be married in the bosom of her family. And I can wait a week!"

"A week!"

The waiter interrupted with eggs Benedict. Betsy asked hurriedly, "What are we going to do this afternoon?"

"That," answered Joe, accepting the change of subject, "is a problem. For dinner tonight we're going to a little French restaurant down in Greenwich Village and then, of course, you must see the Great White Way. But this afternoon—we have such a few hours, and this is such a marvelous mad city! Do you want the Metropolitan Museum? Or a *Thé Dansant*? (I can tango.) Or the Bowery because you're a writer, or Fraunces Tavern because Washington ate there . . . ? Betsy, you're not listening!"

"Yes, I am," she answered happily.

"Then what do you want to see most?"

You! Betsy thought. She couldn't keep her eyes away from him—from the strong, finely-modeled face. His eyes were dancing. His lower lip was thrust out in a reckless way she remembered. "I'll let you plan it," she said demurely, and he grinned at her.

"Then we'll go to Central Park and sit under a tree."

The waiter brought salad, and Betsy asked about the uncle and aunt with whom Joe had lived for a time.

"Uncle Alvin died last spring. I went back to Butternut Center for the funeral. Aunt Ruth is carrying on with the store. I think a lot of Aunt Ruth."

"I'm sorry about Uncle Alvin."

"What's new at 909?" Joe asked. That was his name for the Ray house. After Betsy finished high school, the family had moved from Deep Valley to 909 Hazel Street in Minneapolis.

She talked fast, telling him that her older sister, Julia, who was an opera singer, and Paige, her flutist husband, were in Minneapolis for a visit. Margaret was in high school now.

Joe had already heard Tacy's news.

"What about Tib?" he asked. Betsy, Tacy and Tib had been a threesome ever since childhood when Betsy's short braids, Tacy's red ringlets, and Tib's fluffy yellow curls were always seen together on the Big Hill in Deep Valley.

"She was graduated in June from the art department at Browner. In Milwaukee, you know. She stayed with her grandparents there while she was going through college."

"This war will hit Tib hard," Joe reflected, "because of her German ancestry."

They talked about the war. Joe's heart, like Betsy's, was with the British and the French. His face grew grave when he said there was a great battle raging along a river called the Marne.

"I'm thankful you're home safe," he said.

"Joe," Betsy asked, "did you see me on the *Columbic*?"

"Yes. Don't mention it!" After a silence he added, "But sometime I want to hear all about your trip."

"And I want to hear all about your graduation. Oh, Joe!" Betsy said, and her voice trembled a little. "We have so much to catch up on!"

"We can do it," he answered consolingly, "sitting beside our own fire after we're married."

Feeling her cheeks grow hot again, Betsy looked away—at pink damask walls and glimmering crystal chandeliers.

"Won't it be long enough if we're engaged a week?"

Betsy looked back at him. "Why, we're not engaged yet!"

"But you said—"

"I meant that *after* we got engaged we'd have to wait a while. Joe Willard, you know very well that you haven't even proposed!"

His deep laugh rang out. "Well, I certainly won't do it here!" he said. "So hurry and finish your ice cream and we'll get up to Central Park. Then we must get that ring. Did I tell you I have seven hundred dollars in the bank? And no debts? And a job?"

"That," said Betsy, twinkling, "is the sort of thing you tell my father and not me."

"Gosh!" said Joe. "I'm thankful your father likes me. At least he used to. Do you think he still does?"

She finished her ice cream and coffee and Joe paid the waiter and left a lavish tip. He guided Betsy out of the room, gripping her arm as though she might vanish if he let go.

In another taxicab they rolled up Fifth Avenue, past the fine shops, and the Public Library, and the brownstone mansions in which millionaires lived.

"Many a heroine I have put in those mansions!" Betsy said.

They alighted where Central Park's hilly rectangle of grass and trees and rocks rolled northward, walled in by towering buildings. Near a fountain stood a row of horses hitched to ancient victorias with coachmen in tall hats.

"If I didn't have to propose," said Joe, "we could take a ride through the Park and I'd show you the Zoo and the Shakespeare Garden and the merry-go-round. We'd hire a rowboat and go riding on the lake. Sure you want me to propose?"

"Positive!" said Betsy.

So they found a bench under a tree which was dropping a few yellow leaves. Nursemaids were rolling carriages past, strollers were enjoying the sun, and a vendor was offering grapes and pomegranates and peaches while a hurdy-gurdy played "The Sidewalks of New York."

Joe took Betsy's hand and they smiled at each other.

"It's wonderful to be sitting here together," Betsy said.

"Together!" said Joe. "That's a beautiful word. So much nicer than 'apart.' Aren't you glad we're going to be married next week?"

"Now Joe!" said Betsy. "You know I've been gone from home almost a year. I can't leave Minneapolis right away. . . ."

"That's easy! We can live in Minneapolis."

"But I wouldn't for the world have you give up the *Transcript*!" Betsy cried, distressed. "I'll live in Boston or wherever is best for you, but . . ."

"What I want to do," said Joe, "is earn my living writing. And I'm going to do it sometime. But while I'm on a newspaper, I'd just as soon be in Minneapolis as Boston."

"Would you really?" Betsy cried joyfully. "Oh, Joe! And you have such a fine record back there! You wouldn't have a bit of trouble getting a job on the *Tribune* again."

"I could telegraph and get one," Joe said grandly. "The old man told me so when I left. I don't think, though," he added, "that I'll telegraph. I want a good salary. You know . . . I'll be a married man."

Betsy squeezed his hand.

"I'll go back to Boston," Joe planned. "I'll resign, pack my bags, and come out to Minneapolis. Wedding a week from today?" he questioned briskly, looking down.

Betsy burst into laughter. "You still haven't proposed!"

"Well, there isn't time now! Tiffany's will be closing." He jumped up but he sat down again.

"Wait a minute, Joe!" said Betsy, her voice serious. "Let's save our seven hundred dollars for your trip out, and renting an apartment, and buying furniture. I don't want an engagement ring. I don't care a thing about it."

"But I do. I want to buy you a ring and I want to buy it at Tiffany's."

A little smile crossed her face. "You might," she suggested innocently, "buy me a wedding ring?"

"By Golly!" cried Joe. "What a woman I'm marrying! That's exactly what I'll do!"

Hands swinging, they ran for a taxi, and in spite of late afternoon traffic, they were soon in spacious, haughty Tiffany's.

A clerk in a frock coat showed them trays of rings which Joe inspected critically. He acted, Betsy thought admiringly, as though he bought a wedding ring every day.

Wide bands, the regal clerk disclosed, were going out of fashion. Narrow bands were coming in. Platinum was much used.

"I like gold better," Betsy said timidly, and he measured her finger for a slender gold band. She put it on.

Joe took her hand. He turned it this way and that, judicially, as though the soft white hand weren't Betsy's and the ring their wedding ring.

"Do you like it, Betsy?"

"I love it."

The young man put it in a velvet-lined box which Joe dropped nonchalantly into his pocket. But back on Fifth Avenue he took it out and tore off the wrappings. He put the ring on Betsy's right hand, and lifted her hand swiftly, and kissed it.

"Oh, Betsy!" he said.

They boarded a double-decker bus—Betsy had loved them in London. They sat on a top front seat with Betsy's head on Joe's shoulder, and the hand with the ring on it spread out for both to admire. Ahead in the strip of sky between the city's buildings were thin banners of pink and great thick banners of mauve. It was an evening for banners.

At Washington Arch they put the ring back in its box and came down to terra firma. Skirting the north side of Washington Square, they turned into a maze of narrow twisting streets, of old houses and foreign-looking shops, and stables made over into studios. Betsy looked around delightedly. This, Joe said, was Greenwich Village where writers, artists, and musicians lived.

Chez Minette was in a basement. It was a place Joe came to often when he was in New York. Minette, short and stout in a tight black dress, sat at the cashier's desk. She greeted him with laughter.

"Ah, *m'sieu*! Tonight you make the *crêpes suzettes* again? It was droll, mademoiselle, when he came out to the kitchen! My husband attached to him an apron!" She dabbed at dewy eyes.

"Joe!" cried Betsy. "Can you really make *crêpes suzettes*?"

"Superb ones!" he grinned. "But not tonight. I'll toss some up when we're having company some night. Minette, permit me to present my fiancée."

"Ah, *la chère petite*!" cooed Minette, embracing Betsy. And when Joe and Betsy were seated, side by side, at a table with a red-checked cloth and a fat red candle in the center, he said triumphantly, "There! Our engagement is announced!"

They talked long and gaily over hors d'oeuvres, soup, roast chicken, and salad. Minette beamed on them but she did not interrupt even when a smiling waitress brought *crêpes suzettes* for dessert. Guests came and went. The candle burned low, and Joe's high spirits also flickered down.

"We'll have to leave," he said at last, looking at his watch. "I do want you to see Broadway at night—that glaring white light, and the crowd moving slow as molasses up and down. It's hard to let you go, though. But it's all decided; isn't it? We'll be married as soon as I get there?"

"As soon as I can manage it," Betsy amended. It wouldn't be easy, she knew, to persuade her family to such haste.

Joe held her hands closely in both of his, and he looked at her with an earnestness she had never seen before in his blue eyes.

"Betsy," he said, "I've been lonely for you these last three years. I was a pretty solitary kid, as you know, after my mother died. But I was never lonely. I was always self-sufficient. And after we fell in love I felt so warm and happy. But I should never have left you and gone away to Harvard . . ."

Betsy interrupted. "Why, Joe!" she cried. "What a thing to say! I was the one who failed, acting so silly and frivolous. But I never cared for anyone but you. Not for a moment!"

Joe did not answer that. He was silent for a long time.

"Betsy," he said at last, "I love you. I love you from that cloudy dark hair clown to your slender feet. I love your eyes, and your soft hands, and your sweet voice, and the way your laugh chimes out. Everything about you is enchanting to me. But Betsy, it's lots more than that."

He seemed to be thinking out loud.

"I can always talk to you," he said. "I can make plans, or puzzle out ideas, or build castles in the air. I don't need to think what I'm saying or guard my words. You understand my high moods and my low ones. You understand *me*, I guess.

"I want to be married to you and have you around all the time. I want to come home to you after work and tell you about my day. I want to hear you humming around, doing housework. I want to support you. I want to do things for you. If we were married and I was coming home to you tonight, I wouldn't care if we had just bread and milk.

"You know, Betsy, we never quarrel when we're together.

We never will, I really believe, when we are married. But if we aren't, something might come between us again.

"Betsy, you fit into my life as perfectly as a rose fits its stem. You and I match like the pieces of a broken coin." After a long pause, he said, "Love me always, Betsy! I have given my whole heart to you."

Betsy could not answer for a moment because her eyes and throat were full of tears. The restaurant was empty, except for Minette who was counting money busily into a long black bag. Betsy leaned close and put her wet cheek against Joe's.

"I love you, too. Just the way you love me. And we'll be married. I promise."

3
OBJECTIONS

When Betsy pushed up the shade and looked out the window of her berth on the second morning after leaving Joe, the train was running alongside a mighty river. A wide sweep of cold living water surged between rocky cliffs to which pines and white birches were clinging in a pallid light.

It was the Mississippi!

"Minnesota, hail to thee!" Betsy whispered, staring out. Then she pulled her underwear out of the hammock swinging beside her berth. For since they were following the river they would soon be reaching St. Paul. And then came Minneapolis!

Her family would be waiting at the station. And 909 would be shining. Her father always joked that her mother scoured the coal scuttle when the children came home from a journey. There would be a fire in the grate if it were cool enough, and flowers everywhere, and delectable odors floating from the kitchen.

"Don't you dare eat breakfast!" Mrs. Ray would warn a traveler returning home in the morning. "Well, just a cup of coffee, maybe, if you want the fun of going to the diner! But breakfast will be waiting for you here."

Betsy could imagine the culinary splendor that would be waiting for her after a trip to Europe. Fried chicken, probably! Or sausages and scrambled eggs! Anna's muffins, and the choicest jams and jellies her mother had put up over the summer.

In kimono and boudoir cap, with toilet kit in hand, she went to the ladies' dressing room. Removing the cap, she frowned at a crop of curlers. "Whatever am I going to do about curlers after I'm married!"

But the problem was lost in the rapturous thought of her engagement. She would not tell her family until evening, she planned. She did not want such glorious news lost in the hubbub of homecoming. Besides, it would take tact to reveal Joe's plans.

By the time she was clad in her Paris suit and hat, the train was in St. Paul. The wait there seemed interminable. Then they were on their way again. The porter brushed her and was tipped. He began to stack luggage out in the vestibule.

Betsy took up her handbag, camera, umbrella, and the mummylike package that held Tacy's doll. She was first in the line that started forming in the aisle. At last came the longed-for "Minneapolis!" The train slowed to a stop and, hidden behind a mountain of baggage, Betsy looked out to see a family portrait:

Her father, tall, portly, and erect, his straw hat in his hand, his hair thin and silvery above a face beaming with calm happiness.

Margaret, trim, dainty, and equally erect, beside him. She looked like a young lady, in skirts to her shoetops. She wore her hair, like Tacy's, in coronet braids.

Julia's smile poured out love and joy and eager welcome. Small but stately, with the carriage and manner of a singer, she clung to the arm of her tall young husband, Paige, and searched the train windows for Betsy's face.

Red-haired Mrs. Ray seemed to be shooting out sparks of excitement. In a smart green suit and jaunty hat with pheasant feathers, she looked like another girl.

They were all there, as Betsy had known they would be, except Anna, the hired girl, and she would be frying the chicken. The porter opened the door, and Betsy flew into their arms—home at last, out of the Great World and into this small, cozy, dear one!

The Rays kissed and hugged and wept. They talked and laughed and interrupted one another. Betsy's bags were collected and the party crowded into a taxicab. Paige sat with the driver but he kept looking around, quiet and smiling.

"Oh, how homesick I was!" Betsy wailed.

"Poor darling!" crooned Mrs. Ray.

"Darn fool girls!" grumbled Mr. Ray. "Getting married! Going to Europe! Only Margaret has sense enough to stay home."

"What's in that big bundle?"

"A doll for Tacy's baby."

"But how can you know it's going to be a girl?"

"Tacy couldn't have anything but a nice, quiet, little girl!"

"How's Joe?" Julia asked.

"Fine! Fine!" Betsy tried to sound offhand.

Mr. Ray wanted news of the war. "Teddy Roosevelt and his Rough Riders could soon straighten things out."

Talk was still gushing when the cab stopped. Betsy gazed out at a gray stucco bungalow, gay with striped awnings and flowers still bright in window boxes around a glassed-in porch. The porch was covered with reddening vines which her father had transplanted from their home in Deep Valley.

"Stars in the sky!" cried Anna from the doorway, and Betsy flew up the steps. Anna had changed. The knob of hair atop her head was gray, and her broad, kind face looked thinner.

"We were lonesome for you, lovey!" She wept as they hugged.

"Well, she's home, Anna!" Mr. Ray said with satisfaction. "What's more, she's going to stay a while."

"She isn't going to stir from 909 for months and years!" Mrs. Ray cried gaily.

They swarmed into the wicker-and-cretonne-furnished porch. Betsy rushed for the chaise longue where she used to love to lounge and read. She flung herself down.

Jumping up, she spun through double doors into the living room, which had dark woodwork, leaded-glass panes, and a soft, green, oriental rug. At one end rose a small platform with a full-length mirror which reflected the stairway. At the other, the fireplace was flanked by bookcases, with niches above for photographs and the goldfish bowl. Her father's leather chair stood near. Betsy ran to hug it.

Margaret hurried from the kitchen lugging a huge fluffy cat. "This is Kismet. He jumps up on Papa's chair, and then up to the bookcase, and drinks from the goldfish bowl."

Julia dropped down at the piano and started to play, "You're Here, and I'm Here, so What Do We Care?" and

Mr. Ray stood with his arm around Mrs. Ray, beaming. Anna pounded a brass gong.

"Remember, Julia," Betsy cried as they all pushed out to the dining room, "how Anna used to bang that gong for breakfast? But I never could get you up."

"Nobody else can either," Paige remarked.

The table was laid with place mats and the best china and silver. And there *was* fried chicken, and there *were* muffins!

"Did you have them, Margaret, on the first day of school?" Betsy asked. "Why aren't you in school today?"

"Because you came home from Europe."

"You notice," Mr. Ray said, "I'm not at the store."

"Paige and I," Julia remarked, "ought to be in New York this minute but we wouldn't leave until you got home."

"I should think not!" Mrs. Ray said, pouring coffee from the silver pot.

As soon as breakfast was over, Betsy brought out her presents.

"Lovey, it's puny!" Anna exclaimed, putting on a pink enameled pin. "Puny" was Anna's word for "beautiful."

The Rays admired, paraded, cried their thanks, while Kismet rattled tissue paper and darted fiercely at ribbons. It was like Christmas morning in the Ray living room when Tacy burst in.

"Where's that indefinable Paris air?" she shouted, as Betsy ran to hug her, but she was careful not to hug too hard for Tacy's usually graceful body looked large and cumbersome.

Julia, at the piano again, began the "Cat Duet."

"What's going on here?" Paige demanded as Betsy and Tacy howled and yowled in unison.

"They sang it all the way through school," Margaret explained with the soft amusement her sisters always roused in her.

Betsy tore herself away. "Here, my Titian-haired friend! See what I brought your child!"

Everyone watched expectantly as Tacy unwrapped the package. A pink plume showed, then flaxen curls, a pale blue dress, and pink gloves, shoes, and stockings.

"Wait till Harry sees this!" Tacy laughed. "He's already bought his son a baseball mitt."

"We'll fool Harry!" Betsy cried.

But Mr. Ray shook his head in warning. "Harry Kerr almost always gets his own way."

Julia wanted to dress Betsy's hair in the new French roll. "The idea of your coming home from Europe wearing your hair the same way you wore it when you left!"

Betsy obligingly pulled out the pins, and Julia was brushing and twisting when a tall exuberant girl came in. During the last year Louisa Hilton had become Margaret's inseparable friend. She called Margaret Bogie and Margaret called her Boogie.

"I can't believe it!" Betsy whispered to Julia, for Margaret was the dignified one. Her sisters nicknamed her The Persian Princess.

Boogie stayed for lunch, and so did Tacy. Neighbors started dropping in. Betsy's trunk arrived. She settled her belongings in her blue and white bedroom, furnished with bird's-eye-maple furniture which she had inherited when Julia got married. Tacy helped her, while the others came in and out.

"Where's Tib?" Betsy asked.

"Back in Deep Valley. In the chocolate-colored house." That was their name for Tib's home which had seemed like a mansion to them when they were children. "She wants to work here in Minneapolis this winter," Tacy added.

"Oh, wouldn't that be scrumptious!"

"What did you do in New York?" Julia wanted to know, for Julia loved New York. And Betsy told them about lunch at the Waldorf and dinner in Greenwich Village, but she did not tell her secret.

She told it to Tacy, though, when Tacy left and Betsy walked with her down to the corner. She almost always told her secrets to Tacy.

"Joe and I," she announced abruptly, "are engaged."

"Betsy!" Tacy threw her arms around her. "Oh, I'm so glad! I was afraid it hadn't happened when you told us about New York. You acted so cool and collected."

"Cool and collected!" Betsy laughed, hiding a hot face in Tacy's shoulder. "I'm in a daze. I'm in a dither. I can't take it in."

"When are you going to be married?"

"Soon," Betsy answered. "Very soon."

She worried a little about that, walking back in the smoky September twilight. She had known all along that her father wouldn't like Joe's haste. And this talk about missing her so much, about her not leaving home . . . that made things hard.

But after dinner her father lighted a fire in the grate, and they all gathered in the dancing light—Paige and Julia on the couch, Betsy in a worn cherry-red bathrobe near her mother, and Margaret, with Kismet, on the floor beside her father, who was stretched out in his leather chair, his feet on a footstool, smoking. Betsy knew that the time had come.

"There's something I haven't told you folks," she began slowly, and stopped.

"It's about the war!" Mrs. Ray exclaimed.

"I hope you didn't run out of money," Mr. Ray said.

"Bettina!" cried Julia, her voice thrilling. "You're engaged!"

"Yes, I'm engaged to Joe." Betsy's smile broke through and everyone fell upon her with tender cries and kisses.

"You two were made for each other! Oh, Paige, isn't it wonderful?" sang Julia.

"I'm very happy for you, dear," her mother said. "But Betsy! You'll be living in Boston!" Mrs. Ray's voice took on a tragic note.

"You don't need to worry about that, Mamma," Betsy answered, radiant. "Joe is planning to come back to Minneapolis. He's going to get a job here."

"When will the wedding be?" asked Margaret, starry-eyed.

"Well," Betsy answered, "I want to talk that over." She smiled, but the smile looked anxious. "Joe wants to be married very soon."

"Why, that's all right! Isn't it, Bob?" said Mrs. Ray. "We can announce it as soon as you are rested from your trip. Would you like a bridge or a tea—for the announcement party, I mean?" Mrs. Ray looked businesslike as she always did when planning a party.

"There wouldn't be time for parties," Betsy replied. "When Joe says 'soon' he means 'soon.'"

"But you . . ." Her mother paused. "What do you think about that?"

"I wouldn't mind. I wouldn't mind at all."

"What about the job in Boston?" Mr. Ray asked, puffing.

"He's given that up." Betsy drew a deep breath. "He'll be here next week—to be married."

Mr. Ray put down his cigar. He looked displeased. "But he'll have to get a job first."

"Now, Papa!" Julia said soothingly. "You remember how long Joe worked on the *Tribune*? He won't have any trouble getting a job there."

"Probably not," Mr. Ray agreed, "though there's a new setup on the *Tribune*. New editor, I believe. But Joe does have to have a job. Marriage isn't all love and kisses, Betsy."

"Oh, we know that!" Betsy cried eagerly. "That's the reason I haven't an engagement ring. Joe wanted to go to Tiffany's and buy me a diamond as soon as I got off the boat. But we realized we needed our money to rent an apartment and buy furniture. So we only bought a wedding ring."

"A wedding ring!" His voice was shocked.

"Oh, dear!" said Mrs. Ray. "That does sound serious! And you're barely home, Betsy! You're hardly unpacked!"

"But Mamma!" Betsy cried pleadingly. "I'm going to be living right here in Minneapolis. I won't be going away."

"It won't be the same," said Mrs. Ray, and started to cry.

Mr. Ray spoke in the deliberate manner he always used for family pronouncements.

"I like Joe," he said. "He's a very fine young man. Of course it's three years since I saw him; and three years is a pretty long time. But I feel sure this can all be adjusted when he *asks* to marry you, Betsy." There was a faint but significant emphasis on "asks."

Betsy remembered in a panic the formal letter Paige had written, asking for Julia's hand.

"Oh, he's going to ask you, Papa!" she said hastily. "Don't think he doesn't realize he ought to do that! But he wants to be married so soon! Just the minute he gets here! That's why I thought I'd better explain. So we

34

could be getting ready for the wedding. You know . . . some potted palms and things."

"Potted palms!" Mrs. Ray echoed, and Mr. Ray's expression grew darker, almost forbidding.

"You mean," he said, "that Joe will ask me after he gets here and we've moved in some potted palms and the minister is standing up in front of the fireplace ready to marry you?"

That was exactly Joe's idea, and Betsy didn't know whether to laugh or to cry.

"Before," Mr. Ray went on accusingly, "he even has a job? He's given up the job in Boston, you say?"

"But I thought you'd be pleased about that!" Betsy cried, her voice shaking. "I thought you'd *like* to have us living here in Minneapolis."

"Oh, we do! We do!" Mrs. Ray exclaimed, wiping her eyes firmly. "We want that more than anything. Don't we, Bob?"

"Yes, I'll be pleased with the Minneapolis job—when he gets one."

"Papa!" Betsy's voice was almost angry. She had realized before from which of her parents she inherited her well-known stubbornness. "Can you imagine any newspaper in the whole wide world not giving a job to Joe?"

"Well," said Mr. Ray, irritably, "you're taking in a lot of territory. I'll admit, though, that Joe can probably get a job. And whenever he does I see no objection—after a

proper interval—and if he has saved plenty of money—
and when he and I have discussed the matter—to your
having a beautiful wedding."

"But we don't want a beautiful wedding! That is, it
will be beautiful to us, but we just want to stand up and
be married."

She was near tears, and Julia came to the rescue again.

"Really, Papa," she said brightly, "it's providential!
Paige and I have to go back to New York next week, and
I couldn't bear not to be here for Betsy's wedding."

"Yes," said Mrs. Ray, now entirely on Betsy's side, in
spite of losing a whole procession of parties. "Yes, we
simply have to have Julia, Bob!"

"And Betsy simply has to eat!" said Mr. Ray, extremely nettled. Betsy now was wiping her eyes, and he
relented a little. "We'll talk it all over when Joe comes,"
he added kindly and rose.

Everyone knew what would come next. For in every
family crisis Mr. Ray always did the same thing.

"I'll put on the coffee pot," he said.

He moved majestically out to the kitchen. Kismet
followed, mewing, and Margaret followed Kismet, but
not without a pitying glance at Betsy. Julia and Paige and
her mother gathered around her with comforting whispers. Betsy could not speak.

She felt sure Joe would find a way. He always did.
But the trouble was—so did her father. Her father, with
his inspired suggestions, which he called "snoggestions,"

always made everything right. What happened, Betsy wondered forlornly, when he was on one side and Joe on the other?

"Bob," Mrs. Ray called, "bring some of those sugar cookies, the ones Anna made especially for Betsy."

4

OBJECTIONS OVERCOME

In a week, less a day, Betsy was back in the cavernous railway station waiting for Joe.

At 909 the ritual of preparing for an expected arrival had been performed. The house was polished; there were flowers in the vases; Anna had remembered that Joe liked coconut cake and had made a towering beauty.

The dining room table was laid again with the best place mats, china and silver, and Betsy had asked for sausages and scrambled eggs—and muffins, of course. Joe was staying in a hotel, but Mrs. Ray had insisted upon his coming for breakfast. Betsy was to bring him back in double-quick time.

"No billing and cooing along the way!" Mr. Ray had joked. He must get to the store; Margaret had to go to school; and they didn't want to leave before they had welcomed Joe.

Everyone was talking cheerily about welcoming Joe for it was plain that Betsy was a little subdued. After her father's decision it had been impossible to set a wedding day, or buy a trousseau, or make any plans. Everyone spoke lovingly of her engagement, but no one mentioned her wedding, and Betsy kept remembering the urgency with which Joe had said he wanted that to be soon. She was troubled about Joe, and troubled too about her father, who went around whistling as he always did when he was worried.

But her spirits lifted, waiting beside the tall gates. Back in the city she loved, with the family she adored, she had still longed for Joe—morning, noon, and night.

I'm in love, all right, she thought, smiling.

She was wearing a green plaid skirt with a ruffled white waist, her hands thrust deep in the pockets of a short green coat. And although she looked so casual, she was waved, manicured, perfumed, and her green Gibraltar bracelets jingled as the train rushed in and she sped through the opening gates.

In seconds, Joe was swinging toward her, cane on one arm, a bag in either hand. In seconds, cane and bags were on the ground, and Betsy's new French roll was toppled. She pinned it up, blushing and laughing.

Joe surveyed her. "Wear that skirt on our honeymoon!" he commanded.

They hurried to the line of taxicabs; and one of the drivers, a large, harassed-looking man with gray hair, closed a door upon them.

"909 Hazel Street, skipper!" Joe said. He leaned back and put his arm around Betsy. "Well, I've given up my job! I'm a man of leisure. Nothing to do but get married."

He looked so shiningly happy that Betsy hated to tell her news, but it had to be told.

"Joe," she said, "I'm so sorry! But Papa doesn't like the idea of us hurrying things up. You know how proud Papa is, Joe. He just doesn't like it. Especially since—you haven't asked his consent to our marriage."

"By Jiminy!" Joe replied. He looked both chagrined and amused. "I ought to be ashamed of myself. But just you wait, honey! I'll ask him in style." Not at all perturbed, he leaned over and kissed her.

"But Joe!" Betsy persisted. "That isn't all. He doesn't like it that you haven't got a job."

"Haven't got a job!" echoed Joe. "Why I haven't had time to get one. I just got here."

"I know," Betsy gulped. "And he's awfully pleased, and so is Mamma, that you gave up the job in Boston. But what Papa says is—you ought to have a job before we talk about getting married. That's only good sense, he says. After you get a job, then he and Mamma will announce the engagement, and we can pick out our apartment and our furniture and have a lot of parties—"

Joe leaned forward abruptly. "Make it the *Tribune*, skipper," he said.

Betsy caught his hand and squeezed it joyfully. She had known Joe would straighten everything out!

"That's a wonderful idea!" she cried. "You can get a job there just by asking. There's a new editor, though."

"There is?" Joe turned abruptly.

"That's what Papa says."

Joe stared at Betsy but he did not seem to see her.

"Just watch Willard's smoke!" he muttered to himself.

The driver had turned his car, and they rode back down a morning-fresh Hennepin Avenue to Fourth Street where the *Tribune* and the rival *Journal* offices stood. Joe did not speak; he was frowning; but the slant of his lower lip showed exhilaration in the nut he had to crack.

"Wait here, honey!" he said when the cab stopped. Before she could answer he was through the door of the *Tribune* building and halfway up the stairs.

The cab fare would be high, Betsy thought, but she

wasn't worried. It was worth the money to go home with the announcement that Joe had a job. What concerned her was keeping breakfast waiting.

Oh, they'll think the train was late! she consoled herself, but she watched the door of the building eagerly, waiting for Joe to come bounding out with a triumphant smile.

When he emerged, however, he wasn't smiling. He came to the cab and spoke crisply—to the driver, rather than to her.

"Wait a little longer. I'm going into the *Journal*," he said. Cane on arm, he swung boldly up the street.

Betsy looked after him feeling half-scared but she was interested, too, in his single-minded drive. Was this the way he went about a newspaper assignment? Was this what he was like out in that world she did not know?

Well, whatever had happened at the *Tribune*—the new editor, of course!—he would soon have a job on the *Journal*. She still refused to think of the cab fare but a vision of her waiting family would not be banished.

She spoke with dignity to the large slumping back of the driver. "I'm going to telephone my mother."

He turned and glanced down at Joe's bags. "All right, miss," he answered gruffly and Betsy found a drug store telephone.

"What is it, darling? Was the train late?" her mother asked.

"Not that. We'll explain when we get there."

"Well, hurry! Anna has the muffins ready to pop in the oven, and Papa's getting hungry."

"We won't be long now."

Betsy reached the cab just as Joe did.

"I was phoning the family to tell them we'd be late," she began, but again she could see he wasn't listening.

"The *Courier*!" he said to the driver.

To her, during the short ride he said nothing at all. He did not look at her nor even seem to know that she was there, but Betsy understood. He had ruled out every thing, even her, in the strength of his determination.

He would soon run out of newspapers!

Waiting in front of the *Courier* building, she did give the cab fare a thought. But she tossed it away. With Joe fighting like this, she had better things to think of—and to do.

"I'm going to telephone my mother again," she told the driver's back.

"Betsy!" Mrs. Ray wailed. "What's the matter?"

"I haven't time to explain. I just want to ask you please to go ahead with breakfast. Joe and I will put on the coffee pot whenever we get home."

"But Betsy! The table looks so lovely. I can't bear . . ."

"We can't help it," Betsy said. "Please, Mamma! Please!" and she put down the receiver.

This time she got back to the cab ahead of Joe, and he was gone so long that she began to grow hopeful, but when he came out she knew at once that the news was not good.

He strode forward with his usual vigor but it was like the vigor of a sleepwalker. He was not discouraged because he would not be discouraged. And if he was afraid, the fear was held deep down and not allowed to come up. He had closed his mind against any possibility of failure. He was going to get a job!

He jumped into the cab and said to the driver, "The Marsh Arcade."

The Marsh Arcade! Betsy thought to herself. Why was he going to that group of fashionable little shops? There were a few offices on the upper floors, she remembered, but could one of them hold a job for Joe?

It must! And she started praying. She prayed all the way up Nicollet Avenue to Tenth Street. There they reached the Arcade and Joe disappeared inside the swinging doors.

The driver turned around. "There's a foot doctor in that building," he said sourly. "But if your young man always uses taxicabs this way, he can't be looking for a foot doctor."

"Of course he isn't!" Betsy answered warmly. "He's looking for a job."

"A job, eh? Isn't this sort of an expensive way to do it?"

"We want to get married," she confided.

"Well, wait till he lands that job!" the driver advised.

Just like her father! Betsy thought.

"He'll get one," she said.

The seamy face softened a trifle. "I'll say this for him, miss. He isn't letting any grass grow under his feet."

The wait this time was the longest of all. It was very long. But at last Joe pushed through the swinging doors again, and his smile seemed to shed a glow on everything about him—the yellow hair, the dancing eyes, the now triumphant slant of his lower lip.

"Wait a sec!" he called and darted into a florist's shop on the main floor of the Arcade. He came out with an enormous paper-wrapped spray.

"For your mother," he said, climbing into the cab. "909 Hazel Street, skipper. You may now," he added to Betsy, "gather kith and kin for the wedding. I have a job."

The taxi driver heaved around. "That's getting a hit in the clutch, kid!"

"It's the Ty Cobb in me." Joe winked, and he toppled Betsy's French roll again.

"But what is the job?" she demanded, pink-cheeked, pinning up her hair. "There isn't any newspaper published in the Marsh Arcade."

"There's a publicity office," answered Joe. "A fine one."

"Begin at the beginning!" Betsy ordered.

"In the first place," Joe complied, "eight in the morning is no time to be looking for a job. It's almost the busiest spot in the day. I knew that, but I was desperate. My practically-father-in-law saying I was out of a job!

"At the *Trib* and *Journal* I couldn't even get to the

45

city desk. I just filled out forms in the reception room. *The Deep Valley Sun*, the *Wells Courier News*, the *Minneapolis Tribune*, and the *Boston Transcript*."

"And Harvard!" bounced Betsy. "You told them about Harvard, didn't you?"

"You bet I did! I almost told them about you. And when my application blank reached Hawthorne, the city editor of the *Courier*, he must have sort of liked the looks of it, because he sent me to an office his wife runs. The Hawthorne Publicity Bureau. It's starting a big campaign to raise money for the Belgians."

"Joe, how wonderful!"

"And, Betsy, this Mrs. Hawthorne is a charmer!"

"A charmer?" asked Betsy doubtfully.

"An absolute charmer!" Joe replied. "She's tall and dark—a vibrant sort of woman."

"About how old?" Betsy sounded cautious.

"Gosh, I don't know! Ageless! And Betsy, we got to talking, and the first thing I knew, I'd told her all about you and—I hope you won't mind—I asked her to our wedding."

"Joe!"

"Yep, and she accepted. For herself and her husband and their little girl. I told her especially to bring the little girl."

"But you know, Joe, even with the job . . ."

"I know." Joe turned serious. "I think, Betsy, that your father will see things our way. But if you'd like to wait a while, have all those parties and things—why, honey, I'm yours on any terms." He smiled down at her. "Personally, I've waited long enough."

"So have I," said Betsy.

"And just on the chance," Joe went on, "I told Mrs. Hawthorne that I'd rather not start work until Monday. That gives us three days for a honeymoon, if we're married tomorrow. . . ."

"Tomorrow!" cried Betsy.

"Tomorrow!" chortled the driver. "I told you, miss, that he didn't let any grass grow under his feet."

They were all laughing when they drove up to 909, and the fare the driver named wasn't so huge as Betsy had feared. Joe dug down for a magnificent tip.

"A wedding present in reverse, skipper," he said. He and Betsy ran up the steps and the family burst out the door in welcome. Any annoyance over the long wait melted away as Joe kissed Mrs. Ray and gave her the flowers, and kissed Julia, and was introduced to Paige. Margaret had had to leave, but Mr. Ray had stayed home, and his liking for Joe caused his face to brighten.

"You haven't changed," he said in a pleased tone as they shook hands.

"Anna is keeping some muffins hot," Mrs. Ray said.

"Anna," said Joe, "will you do something else for me?"

"Sure, I will."

"Keep those muffins hot just a little while longer," he

begged with an irresistible smile. "I want to talk with Mr. Ray . . . if you have a few minutes, sir?"

"Why, of course, Joe!" But Mr. Ray's tone was stiff again. He led the way upstairs to a small back room which he called his study. It held a roll-top desk and a picture of the shoe store in Deep Valley and an even bigger picture of ex-President Theodore Roosevelt. He and Joe disappeared inside.

The others clustered around Betsy.

"Where under the sun were you?"

"It was pretty awful, waiting."

"Of course, we knew you had a good reason."

"Oh, we did!" Betsy laughed softly. "Joe was looking for a job. And he got it!"

"The *Tribune* took him on!" Mrs. Ray sighed with satisfaction and relief.

"No, the Hawthorne Publicity Bureau. It's run by the wife of the city editor of the *Courier*. She needed a very good man to raise money for the Belgian refugees, and of course she snapped Joe up. And Mamma! He asked her to the wedding."

"The *wedding*!" Mrs. Ray looked alarmed. "But Betsy, even though Joe has a job, you know how Papa feels. . . ."

"I know," Betsy answered soberly. Everything would depend, she thought, on how that interview in the study was progressing.

Everyone had the same thought, and they sat in silence, listening. They heard a steady flow of voices. Joe and Mr. Ray. Joe and Mr. Ray. Joe for a long time, and then Mr. Ray for a long, long time, sounding excited and positive.

Once an intelligible phrase floated out. "Leave it to Teddy!" Mr. Ray was saying.

The group downstairs looked at each other in complete mystification. What, their raised brows seemed to ask, did Teddy Roosevelt have to do with Betsy's wedding?

"Politics!" Mrs. Ray said scornfully.

Anna brought Betsy a cup of coffee. She brought her a muffin. Mrs. Ray and Julia wanted coffee, too, and Paige started pacing the floor. At long last the door of the study opened.

"T.R. is as right as rain," Betsy heard her father declare as he and Joe came down the stairs.

Mr. Ray beamed at the huddled group. "What are you women wasting time for?" he asked jovially. "There's plenty to be done around here, if we're having a wedding tomorrow."

"Tomorrow!" everyone cried out as Betsy and the taxi driver had done.

"Why, didn't Betsy tell you that Monday Joe starts his new job, helping those wonderful Belgians? He and Betsy are entitled to a little honeymoon, aren't they?"

Betsy fled to Joe's arms.

"I told him, Jule," her father continued, "that I felt I could speak for you. I told him we both realized that he and Betsy had known each other for years and ought to know their own minds. They've waited long enough! Especially with this war business on. We may be in that ourselves, if it hangs on. Jule!" His voice warmed with interest. "Joe interviewed Teddy just a short time ago. He's been giving me all Teddy's views. Teddy thinks just as I do, and just as Joe does, that this is an assault on civilization. . . ."

Mrs. Ray was gasping. "But tomorrow! Couldn't it be next week? One day—for a wedding dress and cake and decorations . . ."

Mr. Ray gave Joe a tolerant glance which said: "These women!"

"You only need to organize things," he replied indulgently. "I'll go over to the florist and get him to work on some decorations. How about a wedding bell over the fireplace?" Mr. Ray smiled. "We were married under a wedding bell; weren't we, Jule? And it took pretty well."

"You and I, Mamma," said Julia, "can take Betsy downtown and help her buy a dress. Maybe we could pick Margaret up at school? She ought to be in on this. Anna can do everything that needs to be done here. You'll have a caterer make the wedding cake, won't you?"

"She *will* not," came Anna's voice from the doorway. "I may be getting old, but I can still bake cakes, and decorate them, too. I made the cake when the McCloskey girl was married!"

The McCloskeys were an almost mythical family for whom Anna had worked in the distant past. Any mention of them always served to quell the Rays.

"I'll take Joe to call on Dr. Atherton," said Paige. Dr. Atherton was the Episcopal clergyman who had married him and Julia. "We have to get a license, too, boy!"

Joe did not reply. Betsy's head was on his shoulder. His cheek was on her hair.

"Hey!" Mr. Ray called. "Hey, you kids! Do you want to get married, or don't you?"

Joe and Betsy came back from some deep dream. They smiled at each other, and out at the smiling faces.

"Yes, sir. Certainly. Sure," Joe said hazily.

"Yes, Papa!" chimed Betsy.

5
THE WEDDING

On the morning of her wedding day, Betsy woke early. She lay snugly under the blankets looking around the dim, familiar room and out through a misty filigree of branches at a world still indistinct.

Everything was ready for the great event. This had not been accomplished easily. After Joe and Betsy came out of their daze, the preceding morning, and began to plan, they had promptly run into difficulties.

Paige would be best man and Julia matron-of-honor. That was understood. But when Betsy started blithely naming bridesmaids, her mother had protested.

"Darling, you can't have bridesmaids at a small wedding like this!"

"But Mamma! Tacy couldn't have Tib and me for bridesmaids! The three of us ought to be together in *one* wedding," Betsy had argued.

"Then Tib will have to have a big wedding. You wouldn't! Remember? Besides, Tacy couldn't do it just now."

"That's right! But I'd like Margaret to be something."

"Margaret," said Mrs. Ray, "will be my right-hand man, as usual. And there will be plenty to do, even though it *is* just a family wedding."

"Of course," Betsy hinted, "Tacy and Tib are family."

"Well, practically!"

"And Katie and Leo." Katie was Tacy's sister.

"They've moved to Duluth."

"And Carney and Sam are family," Betsy pleaded, for Carney was almost as old a friend as Tacy or Tib, "Besides, we'll need Carney to play the wedding march."

"That's true," Mrs. Ray admitted.

"And Cab! Cab's certainly family. Remember how he used to stop in for breakfast on the way to high school, Papa?"

Mr. Ray chuckled. "I certainly do."

Betsy had kept on talking rapidly. "Alice is family, Mamma. I've known her all my life. And Winona, and Dennie, and Irma . . ."

"Betsy! Betsy!" Mrs. Ray broke in. "We'll stop with Cab or there'll be no stopping at all."

Joe looked sheepish. "I've invited the Hawthornes, Mrs. Ray."

"They're very welcome," Mrs. Ray said warmly. "And now we must do our phoning, for we have to get downtown."

Betsy smiled, lying in bed, to remember that wild telephoning. After her mother had invited the uncles, aunts, and cousins, Betsy began. With Joe at her elbow, she had called Tacy first, then Carney. Sam, her husband, had been transferred to Minneapolis, and they lived with a baby daughter just a few blocks away.

"What do you want me to play?"

"Why, Lohengrin."

Joe pushed Betsy aside. "Dum, dee, dee, dum," he hummed.

"Would you like 'Song Without Words,'" Carney asked, "for that fateful moment when you're waiting to come downstairs?"

They telephoned Butternut Center, but Aunt Ruth could not come. Homer, her helper in the store, was ill.

"I'll come down to see you soon. Bring my wife," Joe told her grandly.

They telephoned Deep Valley. Tib's light excited voice floated through the room like Tib herself.

Cab had a surprise for them. "Sorry! I'd love to come to your wedding, Betsy, but I have to go to my own."

"Cab! Do I know her?"

"No. She's a North Dakota girl. You'll love her, though."

"Oh, I'm so glad!" Betsy said. It seemed beautifully fitting that she and Cab, friends of so many years, should have the same wedding day.

Betsy had telephoned Mrs. Hawthorne. It wasn't easy, but she summoned her poise for Joe's sake, and the rich joyous voice at the other end of the line reassured her.

"Do you really want us? We'd love to come. I don't know why it is, but I feel already as though I knew your Joe."

Then Mr. Ray had departed for the florist. But before Joe and Paige left to see Dr. Atherton, Joe had called Betsy aside.

"Where shall we go on our honeymoon?" he asked. "We haven't time to go far. Shall I make reservations at a hotel right here in Minneapolis?"

"How about Lake Minnetonka?" Betsy whispered. "I'd like the country better. Wouldn't you?"

"Of course. And there are hotels at Minnetonka. What a woman I'm marrying!" He kissed her.

"Enough of that!" called Paige. "Find out what flowers she wants for her bouquet."

"Anything, and forget-me-nots," said Betsy.

"I'm never going to forget you, honey."

"I just want to be sure."

"Forget-me-nots," said Paige, "may be hard to find at this season."

"If Betsy wants them, I'll find them," Joe replied. He was in his sea-swimming, mountain-toppling mood.

"We'll have Bachelors' Dinner at Shiek's," Paige said. "I'll round up Harry and Sam. That will keep us out from underfoot."

For Anna had poked her head out of the kitchen to say meaningly, "Everyone ate out, the day before the McCloskey girl's wedding!"

Mrs. Ray, Julia, and Betsy were whisked downtown by taxicab. This was no day for trolleys! And they found a lovely dress—almost as fine as a dressmaker could have made, Mrs. Ray remarked. The sweeping white silk was frothy with tulle. It even had long tulle sleeves. And Betsy planned to wear the tulle cap and veil, edged with orange blossoms, that Julia had worn for her wedding.

"You'll wear it next, Margaret," Betsy said, for Margaret had joined them. Julia had phoned the principal in her most impressive voice. After lunch they had all helped Betsy buy silken slips, chemises, nightgowns, a pleated pink chiffon negligee, and a boudoir cap, trimmed with tiny rosebuds.

When they reached home, Mr. Ray was making a fire in the grate. They had picnicked around it.

"Just the five of you! You look like Deep Valley!" Anna had said fondly, looking in.

Everything had been attended to. Everything was planned, or ready. After so many years of loving him, Betsy was going to marry Joe.

She stared out the window where the sky behind the elm trees was streaked now with crimson and gold. She was going to be married tonight, and she wanted her marriage to be perfect.

"Just perfect!" she said softly, aloud.

She wanted her home to be happy and full of love, as the Ray house was. She wanted to be all Joe expected her to be. He knew her well; Betsy was glad of that. She wouldn't have wanted to go through life pretending to be someone she wasn't. He idealized her, though.

Jumping up, she closed the window and found a pencil and paper, and getting back into bed, she made a list. Betsy was always making lists. She had done it for years, resolving at various times to brush her hair faithfully, or to manicure her nails, or to study French, or to read through the Bible.

But I never made a list as important as this one, she thought, writing at the top, *Rules for Married Life*.

1. Handle Joe's money well. That, she knew, was important. She had noticed that married people had more trouble about money than almost anything else. She would keep accounts, she resolved, and never be extravagant—unless Joe wanted to be.

2. Keep yourself looking nice when Joe's around. Don't plaster on sticky creams at night, or wear your hair in curlers. She would put up her hair after he went to work, she planned.

3. Wear pretty house dresses, like Mamma does, and see that they're always clean. Some organdy aprons would be nice, too.

4. Learn to cook. Betsy frowned over that one. *You're fairly bright. You can learn if you try.*

5. Always, always, be gentle and loving. No matter if you're tired or feeling cross. Papa and Mamma don't quarrel, she thought. You and Joe don't need to, either.

She read the list over several times, looking sober. Then she tore it up and, getting out of bed again, she knelt down and pressed her head against the blankets.

Back in bed, she heard her father going downstairs. He would be opening the furnace, for September mornings were cool.

But her wedding day was going to be fair. The sky was already radiantly blue.

Margaret came in, her long black braids hanging over her nightgown. She snuggled into bed beside Betsy.

"I've been thinking!" she said. "When it's time for you to be married, I'm going to put Kismet in the basement. You know how he hops up to that niche above the fireplace to drink out of the goldfish bowl? What if he should do it in the middle of the wedding?"

"Margaret," said Betsy, "you think of everything!"

Julia came in. This was unexpected for, with Julia, getting up was a major undertaking. She came in, blinking sleepily, her curly hair in wild disorder, and climbed in on the other side of Betsy. She closed her eyes.

"Breakfast in bed," she murmured, "would be nice. Golly, it would be nice!"

Betsy and Margaret giggled.

Mrs. Ray came in, crisply dressed. She looked like a general planning a campaign.

"You three get up!" she ordered.

"Mamma," murmured Julia, still with closed eyes, "do I smell coffee, or do I just imagine it?"

"You just imagine it. Get up!"

"It's Betsy's wedding day, you know."

"That's why you have to get up. There's lots . . ."

"I think I hear Papa!" Julia opened her eyes. She cocked her head. She sprang to a sitting position. "Papa!" she cried. "You're an angel!"

"An absolute angel!" Betsy echoed.

"Why do you go and get married then?" asked Mr. Ray, beaming, as he passed a loaded tray. "You stick by us, Margaret!"

Mrs. Ray sat down with a cup of coffee and a slice of buttered toast. "Your father," she observed, "is a man in a million. Don't expect Joe to do this for you, Betsy."

"Joe!" said Betsy with a lilt in her voice. "I wonder how soon he'll be coming."

"Why, not until evening, of course!"

"You won't see him until you meet at the altar."

"Oh, no!" Betsy wailed.

"Someone's coming in now," Margaret observed, trying not to laugh, and Joe hallooed from the foot of the stairs in a loud and happy voice.

"Joe Willard!" Julia called. "You're not allowed to see Betsy until the wedding."

"Bosh!" shouted Joe. "May I come up?"

"No!" cried Betsy, for her hair was still in curlers. She bounced out of bed; and Mr. and Mrs. Ray went down stairs, laughing.

"Maybe Joe could use a cup of coffee," Mr. Ray said.

Joe was drinking coffee when Betsy joined him on the small back porch. He put down the cup to take her hands.

"I have wonderful news! The Minnetonka hotels are closed for the season, but Harry and Tacy have a cottage out there. They'll loan it to us, Harry says."

"Joe!"

"Doesn't it sound like a dream?"

The day passed like a dream. Betsy and Joe sat on the little back porch which was covered with morning glories, still in bluish-pink bloom. They wandered, hand in hand, around the leaf-strewn lawn. They weren't allowed indoors.

Anna was barricaded in the kitchen, beating and stirring and grumbling. The cake was to be a surprise.

The florist carried in potted plants and long cardboard boxes which exuded a wet flowery smell. But the transformed fireplace was to be a surprise, too.

Julia was pressing, for Betsy. Margaret was polishing silver. They kept running out with telephoned messages. Tib had arrived at Tacy's. Carney warned that Sam was buying rice and collecting tin cans.

Joe and Betsy smiled at each other. They had a wonderful getaway plan.

Joe left after lunch. He would not see her now until he saw her coming down the stairs to marry him. He put his arms around her.

"I love you. I could set those words to music," he said, very low.

Betsy was sent upstairs to rest. She went—so she would not see the fireplace—by way of a short flight of stairs that ascended from the kitchen to a landing where it met the flight that came up from the living room platform.

She lay down but she could not rest. It was a good thing, she thought, that she had made her resolutions earlier, for now her head was whirling. She looked around the blue and white room that she would leave so soon.

"I'll be back often. But, as Mamma says, it won't be the same." She could not feel anything but happy, though.

Julia came in to help her pack. She lined a suitcase with tissue paper and folded clothing with exquisite care, slipping in satin sachet bags. Betsy added a worn limp leather copy of Shakespeare's *As You Like It*.

After supper and the early autumn nightfall, she bathed and put on the new silk undergarments, and Julia dressed her hair.

"How many thousands of times you've fixed it for me!" Betsy said.

"You'll be an old married woman when I do it again, Bettina," Julia answered. She and Paige were leaving the next day.

Margaret slipped in, flawlessly dainty in her best blue silk. Beneath the crown of braids, her eyes were sparkling. She held out a box.

"Your bouquet!" she cried. "And there's one for Mamma, and one for Julia, and even one for me!"

Betsy opened it quickly, and he *had* found forget-me nots! Blue and reassuring, they were scattered among pink roses above a shower of white satin ribbons.

Mrs. Ray swept in, gleaming in satin, filling the air with Extreme Violet perfume. While Margaret looked on, she and Julia lifted the snowy wedding dress over Betsy's head. It rustled to the floor, and Julia's deft fingers put the bridal cap in place and spread out the flowing veil.

"Betsy," said her mother, stepping back to gaze, "you look lovely! Go and dress now, Julia! Hurry! And Margaret, get downstairs and turn on all the lights."

She kissed Betsy, and went out, and closed the door.

Betsy stood in the middle of the room. She didn't want to crush her veil by sitting down. The doorbell began to ring. She heard doors opening and shutting, and gay voices, and steps on the stairs.

Margaret would be guiding the ladies to her mother's bedroom and the gentlemen to her father's study. Julia would still be dressing, humming to herself, and surveying effects with a hand mirror. Julia was always late.

A knock sounded. Tacy came in, smiling, and behind her appeared a swirl of golden curls, a doll-like face! Tib flew forward with arms outstretched—but she stopped.

"Betsy! You look so pretty! Much prettier than you are!"

Betsy and Tacy twinkled at each other. "Just like Tib!" their glances said.

"Of course I look pretty!" Betsy cried, shaking Tib and kissing her. "I'm supposed to! I'm a bride!"

"*Liebchen,*" Tib said, "I'm so glad you're back! And about you and Joe! He's exactly right."

Dear little Tib! Betsy thought, when they went out. She must find the right one, too. And then she will have that big wedding. And Tacy and I can be bridesmaids. . . .

It was good to plan someone else's wedding, for, facing her own, her heart was beginning to thump.

Betsy turned to the mirror. She did, indeed, look prettier than she was! The veil was a white cloud around her dark slenderness, her flaming cheeks, and shining hazel eyes.

"I look too happy. Brides are supposed to look shy." But she couldn't manage to look anything but happy.

Margaret, coming up to hurry Julia, darted in. "Kismet's in the basement. I've put paper in the telephone and stopped the chime clock."

Mrs. Ray came up to hurry Julia. "Everyone's here. Papa's pacing the floor, and Joe is almost crazy."

"I'm ready," Julia's voice came sweetly. "Tell Carney she can start." And Betsy heard her mother go downstairs, and the tender melody of "Song Without Words" began to drift upward.

Julia came in, dressed in pale green and carrying violets. She studied Betsy with unhurried attention.

"Carry your bouquet this way, darling. See? You look divine! And go slowly! Remember, they can't start without you." She winked. Then, going to the top of the stairs, she assumed a grave, heavenly expression, and just at that moment came the stirring and familiar strains of the wedding march!

Julia started slowly down the stairs. She turned left at the landing, and disappeared.

Betsy started after her, holding Joe's flowers, the white veil floating behind. She too went slowly, but lightly, on the tips of her toes. She turned at the landing, and descending toward the platform mirror, she glimpsed a gauzy phantom.

She turned again, and faced the crowded room. Her father was waiting, proudly erect, wearing his white vest, and a white carnation on darkly gleaming broadcloth.

Carney sat at the piano. A salmon-pink sash fell over her spreading white skirts. Sam was turning her music.

Dr. Atherton had his back to the fireplace which was quite concealed by fragrant greenery, and golden chrysanthemums, and lighted golden tapers. On one side of a flowery golden bell stood Julia, holding her violets; on the other, Joe and Paige, spruce and pressed, also with lapel carnations.

Joe's blond hair shone. His eyes shone. His lower lip thrust out, of course. Betsy moved forward slowly on her father's arm.

"Dearly beloved . . ." The words of the service came through faintly at first. "We are gathered together here in the sight of God and in the face of this company, to join together this Man and this Woman in Holy Matrimony. . . ."

Joe and Betsy smiled at each other.

"If any man can show just cause why they may not lawfully be joined together, let him speak now, or else hereafter forever hold his peace."

No one spoke.

Betsy heard a long "Wilt thou . . ." and Joe's deep voice answering, "I will." The solemn question came to her. "Wilt thou have this Man to thy wedded husband. . . . Wilt thou love him, comfort him, honor and keep him, in sickness, and in health; and forsaking all others, keep thee only unto him, so long as ye both shall live?"

She heard her voice answering, "I will."

"Who giveth this woman to be married to this man?" She found her hand in Joe's. Then Joe spoke again; then she, herself.

"I, Elizabeth, take thee, Joseph, to my wedded husband, to have and to hold, from this day forward, for better, for worse, for richer, for poorer, in sickness and in health, to love and to cherish, till death us do part . . . and thereto I give thee my troth."

The ring she and Joe had bought in New York was placed on her finger, and in a few moments Joe was kissing her, and everyone was kissing her.

"Mrs. Joseph Willard!" they were saying. How beautiful it sounded!

"I want to meet Mrs. Joseph Willard," came the rich voice she had heard on the telephone, and Betsy found herself greeting a queenly woman with reddish-brown hair, and brown eyes that looked into her own with such warmth Betsy could hardly believe they were meeting for the first time.

Bradford Hawthorne was a small, alert man, with eyeglasses on a humorous face. Little Sally Day—red ringlets and a white lace dress—had the same puckish expression.

Except for the Hawthornes, all the guests were relatives or old, old friends. There was something heart-warming, Betsy thought, about a small wedding like this where everyone knew you and loved you.

Tacy's Irish eyes were smiling around Anna, who was wearing black silk and the pink enamel pin. Tib was laughing delightedly at everyone's jokes. Sam's eyes were crinkled with mischief, and Carney's dimple flashed as she whispered, "He's tied cans to your uncle's car by mistake."

Harry murmured, "Your bags are locked in the Buick."

Joe was gripping Betsy's arm. He did not let go until Margaret called them all to the dining room which swam in the light of more golden tapers. Golden baskets were tied with tulle and filled with yellow roses.

The tables were laden with trembling salads; plates of sandwiches; hand-painted dishes of candies and nuts. Mrs. Ray sat behind the silver coffee pot at one end, and at the other stood Anna's masterpiece—a great gleaming cake trimmed with flowers, ribbons, and a dove!

"Anna! It's too beautiful to cut!" cried Betsy as the crowd gathered around and she poised a silver-handled knife.

"I think the dove is puny," Anna answered, trying to sound modest. "But cut it, lovey! I made it for folks to eat."

Other people ate. Betsy couldn't eat a crumb.

Tib sat on the step coming down from the platform, sketching. "I'm drawing a picture of you, Betsy, so Joe can remember always just how you looked tonight."

"I'll remember," Joe said, but when Tib had finished, he folded the paper and put it in his pocket.

Mrs. Ray spoke casually, loud enough for everyone to hear. "Time to change, Betsy, if you're going to make that train! Why don't you help her, Tacy? And Joe, go get us all more coffee, please."

So Tacy went upstairs, and Betsy followed.

She paused above the platform. Tib, Margaret, little Sally Day, and some girl cousins gathered expectantly below. Betsy took a forget-me-not out of her bouquet and tucked it into her dress. Then the bouquet sailed down, ribbons streaming, and Sally Day caught it and jumped up and down with joy.

Betsy fled up the stairs, but only as far as the landing. With her wedding veil still floating behind, she went down the back stairs to the kitchen. Tacy, in a warm coat, was waiting there. Anna held Betsy's velvet wrap.

Joe came in, followed by Harry, who took Tacy's arm without speaking and sped out the back door. Joe caught Betsy's arm and Anna threw the wrap over her shoulders, but Betsy stopped long enough to give Anna a kiss that belonged—not just to her, but to Betsy's father, and her mother, and her sisters, and the happy Ray house.

The crisp dark had the smell of autumn in it. Chilly stars were looking through the branches. Lights were streaming out of all the windows, and music streamed out, too.

Julia—to help the plot—had gone to the piano. She had begun her father's favorite song:

Believe me, if all those endearing young charms . . .

Everyone was singing.

Tacy was seated beside Harry, at the wheel. He had started the engine of the Buick.

"We can make Minnetonka in an hour," he was saying as Betsy gathered her white veil together beneath the velvet wrap and climbed into the back seat. Joe followed.

But before they rolled away, a shower of rice flew over their heads. They looked out to see Anna, weeping joyfully and waving.

"They threw rice," she shouted, "at the McCloskey girl's wedding. It's for good luck, loveys!"

6
THE GOLDEN WORLD

"You're a very nice wife," Joe announced. "Shouldn't be surprised if I stayed in love with you for a considerable length of time. Say—I want to be reasonable about this—say, a lifetime."

Betsy frowned in thought. "Well," she answered, "since you're being so conservative, I will be, too. I'll stay in love with you for a lifetime, too."

And they went, laughing, into each other's arms, and caught hands, and ran out of their cottage—a rough, unplastered, lakey-smelling cottage, perched on stilts, and painted green. They ran across the lawn which was sprinkled with fallen leaves, and down a steep flight of steps to a dock, stretching out into Lake Minnetonka.

It was the third and last day of their honeymoon. Tonight they would take a streetcar boat to Excelsior where they would catch a streetcar for Minneapolis and the Ray house. Tomorrow Joe would start work at the Hawthorne Publicity Bureau and Betsy would go hunting an apartment.

Last chance for a swim, Joe had said, but Betsy had declared it was too cold. She settled herself in the sunshine on the dock and Joe dropped his towels, flexed his arms, walked to the end, and plunged.

Betsy shivered. "But Joe likes it," she remarked to a gull, posing on a bark-covered post. "My husband likes to swim in icy water."

The gull looked unimpressed.

At the side of the dock was a small wire enclosure used for bait. "But he doesn't like to fish. My husband doesn't like to fish," Betsy told the gull.

He looked scornful.

"My husband," Betsy informed him, "is the handsomest, dearest, cleverest, most wonderful person in the world."

At that, the gull flew away, and Betsy laughed, and

hugged her knees into her arms. She was wearing the green plaid skirt Joe liked, and a middy blouse, with a narrow green ribbon tied around her hair which was dressed in the old way, low and soft around her face. Of course, she had not been able to curl it. But, blessing of blessings, Joe liked it straight!

The water looked like polished green glass—but mobile glass. It came moving toward her, slantwise. The whole great body of the lake came moving toward her, speaking softly, plashing against a rowboat which was moored among the rushes.

The neighboring docks and diving boards were all deserted. So were many of the cottages. The bank here was high and wild, crowded with bronzy undergrowth and trees leaning over the water.

Across the bay, the shore was flat, and there was a boathouse with a little peaked tower. It had an oriental air, Betsy had observed to Joe.

"We must have come to Japan on our honeymoon!"

"I never did trust that Kerr!" Joe replied, and they had laughed as though at scintillating wit.

Betsy turned around and watched him shooting out into the lake. She wished he'd come back.

It was warm, sitting in the sunshine. The weather had warmed up gloriously every day, but the evenings and the mornings had been cold. Joe had sprung up early, while the lake still slept under an eiderdown of mist, to start a fire in the plump air-tight stove. Betsy loved that stove, roaring importantly, gleaming in comic threat through the front damper.

Joe had cooked breakfast—coffee, bacon and eggs, French toast—even sour-milk pancakes. Betsy had breakfasted elegantly in the pink chiffon negligee and the boudoir cap trimmed with rosebuds. But after breakfast she had put on a sailor suit, and one of Tacy's starched aprons, and had washed the dishes, and made the bed, and swept, and brought in bouquets—goldenrod and starry asters, or a spray of thorn-apple berries.

Each morning they had walked to the store, along a road where the trees met overhead, comparing progress on their red and yellow leaves. The roadsides were gaudy with fall growth.

"Those bursting milkweed pods," Joe said, "make me think of grade school. I always expect to be asked to draw them."

"I'll bet your drawings were pinned up on the blackboard."

"They were used to scare the children."

Trying to act like an old married couple, they had bought melons and doughnuts and tomatoes and frankfurters and syrup and milk and crusty bread. The storekeeper, an old Scandinavian woman with bright observant eyes, treated them with great respect.

When they returned, Betsy had tied on the apron again, but Joe did most of the cooking. The kerosene stove was a mystery to her; and, of course, her talents at any stove were meager. Tacy had left a chocolate cake, with fudge frosting half an inch thick, and it proved a boon.

They always lunched on the porch, and sometimes a flicker knocked against the wall.

"You can't come in," Joe would call. "Don't you know this is a honeymoon?"

A little white-tailed rabbit would run across the lawn.

"Don't you know," Joe would ask, "that we're supposed to be left alone?"

The squirrels paid no attention to them. They were busy burying nuts.

In the afternoons Joe and Betsy had sat on their lofty lawn, looking out at the lake which was sometimes cloth of silver and sometimes a carpet of diamonds. They had read aloud—poetry.

"Nothing but poetry is allowed on this honeymoon," Joe had announced on the first day, bringing out a volume of Keats, and one of Shelley, and one of Tagore, and one of Alfred Noyes.

"Shakespeare was a poet," Betsy had replied, producing *As You Like It*. Joe had given it to her one Christmas when they were in high school. He had written on the flyleaf: "We'll fleet the time carelessly as they did in the golden world."

They had read Alfred Noyes the most. Joe had read aloud about the forty singing seamen, and the highwayman who came riding, riding, riding, and "Come back to

Kew in Lilac Time," which Betsy had loved in London, but, especially, "Silk O' The Kine."

Betsy quoted it softly now.

> *. . . her hand lay warm in his clasping hand:*
> *Two young lovers were they . . .*

She thought of those young lovers swimming to their death.

> *Out, far out, through the golden glory*
> *that dazzled the green of the bay:*
> *Two strong swimmers were they. . . .*

Joe was a strong swimmer but Betsy was glad, looking around again, to see that he was headed toward her.

He came up, dripping.

"Colder than blazes!" he said, blowing and snorting and rubbing vigorously. He sat down beside her. "Do you know what I was thinking out there? It would be fun to live in a place like this."

"It would be perfect!" Betsy cried. "Just perfect for two writers! Let's buy that place with the Japanese boathouse."

"All right," said Joe. "Of course, first, I have to earn the money."

"And I have to learn to write things that will sell to the good magazines. Some of my stuff," Betsy admitted, "is pretty awful."

"I'll tell you all old Copey taught us." Professor Copeland had been Joe's favorite teacher at Harvard. "Betsy, maybe you'd do better with a novel. Why don't you try one?"

"Maybe I will," said Betsy, "when we're living out here."

And they began to plan.

"I'll get on a paper when Mrs. Hawthorne's campaign is over," Joe said. "I'll enjoy a stretch of newspaper work. And after a year or so, we'll move out of the apartment and buy a little house—not at the lake yet . . ."

"And have a baby," Betsy put in.

"A boy or a girl?"

"Both. The boy first, so he can take her to parties."

"Let's name the girl Bettina," Joe said. He liked Julia's nickname for Betsy. "And before we settle down, we might travel a bit. New Orleans, California. Have a fling at New York. Would you like that?"

"I'd love it," Betsy answered. "But we won't stay."

"No, we'll come back here to Lake Minnetonka, and write."

It was beautiful sitting on the dock in the sunshine, planning out their lives, but they had to go in. They had to have an early supper, and pack, and row over to the streetcar boat. Harry had said he would pick up the rowboat at the landing there.

They rose reluctantly, and Joe dropped an arm around Betsy's shoulders. They looked up at the wild bronzy bank, the yellowing trees, the little cottage standing sturdily on stilts.

"I hate to leave it," Joe said. "I hate to leave our golden world."

"But our own apartment will be nice," said Betsy. And they climbed the steep stairs, stopping to pick some wild grapes from the flaming vines that loaded the trees.

"I'll get supper," said Joe, when he was dressed.

"All right," answered Betsy. "And I'll pack. But Joe, I'm going to learn to cook. It's the very first thing I'm going to do."

"All I ask," he answered, getting out the bacon, "is for you to learn to make two things: rice pudding and lemon pie."

"Rice pudding and lemon pie," Betsy repeated obediently. "I promise."

Her wedding dress was hanging in the rough damp closet. It looked remote, ethereal, draped in its white veil.

"I'm never going to put it on again," Betsy said dreamily. "Not once! Except, perhaps, for our golden wedding anniversary. Of course, Bettina can wear it for her wedding if she wants to."

"Sentimental!" Joe scoffed. But he looked pleased, and left the bacon to help her fold the dress carefully into a big box which Tacy had remembered to put in the car.

Betsy opened her suitcase and took down the pink negligee. Joe left the bacon again and came over to rub his cheek against hers.

"My pink silk wife!" he said. He liked to say that. After a while he went back to the bacon.

"Shall I pack my husband's things, too?" Betsy asked.

"Certainly. Don't you know your duties as a wife?" he

replied, chopping cold boiled potatoes with the top of a baking powder can. He was very proud of this accomplishment. "I ought to make a sour-cream cake," he remarked, "Leave it for the Kerrs."

But there wasn't time. Supper was hurried. And Betsy washed the dishes while Joe mopped the floor. They wanted to leave the cottage as neat as they had found it.

When they had finished, they put on their wraps, and locked the door, and went down the steps to the rowboat where Joe stowed away the bags. He got the oars and slipped them into the oarlocks.

"I haven't taken one of those streetcar boats for years," he said as they pushed off.

"They're yellow like the streetcars. They're fun. And the streetcars going in from Minnetonka are fun too. They go like lightning, and there's one motorman—or used to be—who puts his hands behind his head and doesn't touch the wheel."

"He's probably been fired by now."

They talked fast and did not look back at the cottage.

The sun had disappeared, and the lake was dull. It was slate-colored, under a slate-covered sky, flecked with pale gray clouds.

A motorboat approached, its prow lifted, throwing out spray. A hunter hailed them, and his boat went on, leaving a widening avenue behind. Waves set the rowboat rocking.

Neither Joe nor Betsy spoke.

When it was quiet again, Joe folded the oars across each other. Moving carefully, he came and sat down beside Betsy. He put his arm around her.

About that time the pink of the afterglow stole into the west. It spread over the sky. It spread over the lake, growing rosier and rosier, and even seemed to tint the gulls who swept back and forth as though reveling in this bath of beauty. The gray clouds became gossamer pink. Joe pointed to one.

"That cloud," he said, "makes me think of you in your pink silk negligee. You're my pink silk wife. You're my wife made out of flowers."

No matter what Joe said, Betsy knew she was just Betsy. But she loved to hear him say these beautiful things. He kept on saying them so long that they almost missed the streetcar boat which took them to the streetcar where they sat on the back seat and held each other's hands.

The motorman drove with his hands behind his head, but Joe and Betsy didn't even notice.

7

THREE RINGS OF A BELL

It was Margaret who found Joe and Betsy their first home.

They had been living for a week at the Ray house—Joe working with great satisfaction at the Hawthorne Publicity Bureau, Betsy dashing all over Minneapolis to look at apartments. She went alone, with her mother, in

Carney's automobile. Tib was now living in town; she had found a job in art-advertising with one of the department stores. But she was too busy to help, and Tacy wasn't feeling well.

"I'll be glad when that baby gets here," Betsy confided to Carney as they drove up and down the autumn-tinted streets. "I'll be glad for Tacy, and, besides, I want to see the little redhead. I know she'll be adorable."

"Of course," Carney chuckled, "she could be a 'he.'"

"Tacy isn't the type for a boy," Betsy answered loftily.

Tacy, too, expected a girl, and the doll Betsy had brought from Germany flaunted her pink plume and yellow curls among the couch cushions in Tacy's living room. Betsy and Carney dropped in there often after the day's hunt was ended.

Day after day, it was a fruitless hunt. Betsy had budgeted Joe's salary of $155 a month—the budget was her department, he had said—and she would not pay more than thirty dollars for rent.

"Not more than thirty," she insisted, "if we have to sleep in the park!"

The search for an apartment at that figure took them all over Minneapolis, and Betsy thought often how beautiful it was—set on the storied Mississippi, glimmering with lakes. A chain of lakes ran actually through the city. Their shores were lined with homes, and even closer to the water lay the public boulevards, scattered with picnickers, fishermen, children with buckets, adventurous masters of sailboats and canoes. Betsy had taken all this for granted once, but not now, remembering the war-stricken cities of Europe.

"How lucky we are to live here!" she exclaimed.

"Nice place to bring up Judy," commented Carney, glancing at a cozy bundle in a basket on the back seat.

When not apartment-hunting, Betsy sat with her mother on the bright glassed-in porch, hemming dish towels. (Mrs. Ray hemmed six to Betsy's one.) After school Margaret and Louisa blew in, the green-and-white ribbons of their high school streaming from their coats.

Blooming, wide-eyed Louisa was always bursting with talk.

"There's nobody, absolutely nobody, left on the football team, Mrs. Ray! And Mrs. Willard, too, of course. That is, if I call you Mrs. Willard. I suppose I do. It seems funny, though. Last year we were champions but everybody graduated. Absolutely everybody! It's simply awful! It makes me feel as though Bogie and I ought to play. I stopped the coach in the hall and asked him why girls couldn't help out in an emergency like this. He seemed surprised, but I mean it! I'm awfully husky, and Bogie is perfectly healthy. Isn't she, Mrs. Ray?"

Louisa paused for breath and gazed at them beseechingly.

Next day it was something else.

"There's a tall skinny boy works in the lunch room. He's crazy about Bogie, Mrs. Ray, and Mrs. Willard. If I call you Mrs. Willard?"

"Oh, please say Betsy!"

"All right, but it doesn't seem respectful. You *are* married, you know. But he just piles gravy on Bogie's roast beef sandwich. Honestly, he does! Mashed potatoes, too. The rest of us don't get a bite, hardly."

"Boogie!" Margaret choked.

"It's true, Bogie. You can't deny it. And I *like* mashed potatoes. Especially with gravy. I get *hungry*...."

"How about some cookies and milk while you're doing your homework?" Mrs. Ray suggested.

Mr. Ray and Joe came home from work, and dinners were jolly. Betsy's father was already Dad to Joe, but Joe and Mrs. Ray had animated discussions about what he should call her: Mother, Mamma, Ma . . .

His preference was for Jule, Mr. Ray's name for his wife, and at last Mr. Ray gave him written permission to use it, sending Margaret for pen and ink while Betsy contributed green sealing wax to make the paper official.

"Stars in the sky!" Bringing in peach cobbler, Anna shook with laughter.

Evenings, they talked around the fire. Her husband and Joe talked war too much, Mrs. Ray declared. The German advance had been stopped at the Marne by a heart-stirring effort of all the French people. Even the Paris taxicabs had rattled up to the front with troops. But the Rheims Cathedral was bombed. A church! An art treasure! It seemed impossible.

That night none of them could talk of anything but war.

Mrs. Ray recalled that her father had fought in the Civil War. And Betsy told a story her grandmother had told her.

"They were living in Indiana, in a log cabin. Grandpa was teaching country school. Lincoln had called for volunteers, but Grandma didn't want Grandpa to enlist. Uncle Keith was only a baby. You weren't born yet, Mamma. One afternoon she saw him coming through their cornfield—tall and thin and redheaded, she said. And he was carrying all the school books in a pile, with the school bell sitting on top. The minute Grandma saw it, she knew what had happened, and she began to cry."

Everyone was silent.

"But she was proud of him, she said," Betsy added.

"And I have the letters they wrote to each other while he was away. Regular love letters!" Mrs. Ray made her tone light for Margaret had jumped up, blowing her nose, and gone to find the cat.

Oftener they didn't talk about war. Betsy told them about Europe, and Joe told them about Harvard, and Mr. Ray told them funny things that had happened at the store. And every evening there were wedding presents to unwrap. Betsy never opened them until Joe came home.

Her parents had given them a set of plated silver. There was a bird in the pattern; Joe and Betsy had picked it out themselves. And they had selected their china, English china, with pink and blue and lilac-colored flowers. Paige and Julia had started them on that. Margaret gave them a statuette of three little monkeys. One was covering its ears, and one its eyes, and one its mouth, and the legend read: *Hear no evil, see no evil, speak no evil.*

"Boogie helped me pick it out. We thought it was funny. And instructive, too," Margaret said.

Tacy and Harry gave them framed prints of two Maxfield Parrish pictures, "Homekeeping Hearts are Happiest" and "The Hanging of the Crane."

Tib sent a cookie jar. "Now learn how to fill it!" she wrote.

The Hawthornes sent a mantel clock. Joe's aunt sent a carving set. Betsy tried to imagine Joe carving at the head of his own table! There were candlesticks from Sam and Carney, a tray from Katie and Leo. There were books and bonbon dishes, vases and jelly spoons, a tea wagon.

"Fine! Fine!" Joe exclaimed. "But where are we going to put all this? Maybe we ought to go up just a little on the rent. Thirty-five, say?"

"Not more than thirty," answered Betsy, "if we look forever."

And it seemed as though they might, indeed, look forever, but on the second Sunday Margaret, who had gone off with Louisa, came into the house with star-bright eyes.

"You know, don't you, that Boogie lives in an apartment? Well, her mother owns the building! And she has an apartment for rent. The people just moved out."

85

"How—how much?" asked Betsy from the couch where she and Joe sat poring over real estate advertisements.

"Twenty-seven dollars and fifty cents!"

"What a sister-in-law!" Joe shouted, whirling Margaret who was trying to act calm. Betsy ran for a hat and jacket.

"And it's just around the corner on Bow Street!" Mrs. Ray cried joyously as Margaret, Joe, and Betsy hurried out.

Louisa was waiting at the foot of the Ray porch. She exploded into speech.

"I thought it was more tactful not to come in. But if you rent it, Betsy, Bogie and I can come in to see you every day after school. We can keep you from getting lonesome. That is, I *imagine* you'll get lonesome. Going away from home all alone with just a husband! Oh, excuse me, Mr. Willard!" she added in confusion as Joe grinned at her.

Bow Street was an old street. The elms were old and had turned yellow and were spattering the lawns with leaves. The houses were old, with spacious porches; and few of the barns had been made into garages. In front of one house, a horse and buggy was hitched.

"It's like Deep Valley," Betsy said, clinging to Joe's arm for he was striding along so fast she could hardly keep up with him.

The apartment building was set on a large elmy lawn. It had an entrance porch with fat fluted pillars, and looked like a large, stone, private house except for sets of triple windows, bulging out.

Oh, I hope we get one of those bays! Betsy thought.

She waited in a rapturous daze while the girls ran to call Mrs. Hilton and Joe walked briskly around the building.

"Looks fine! Looks all right!" he said, returning. His golden eyebrows bristled with excitement.

Bogie and Boogie emerged with Boogie's serene, white-haired mother. They all followed her inside, up a flight of carpeted stairs, to the left-hand back apartment. Betsy calculated quickly. "It will face south and east!"

They entered a small foyer, shiningly empty, but she envisaged a slim table with a silver tray for cards. They turned left into the empty living room, and Betsy ran forward, for at the end was one of those three-winged bay windows. And it looked straight into a yellowing elm tree! Right into the branches!

"Oh, what luck!" she thought. "What luck!"

Joe turned right, into the small kitchen. He returned in a flash to the living room and turned right again, through an archway, into the bedroom. He peeked into the bathroom, and came up to Betsy who was still looking out blissfully into the elm.

She smiled at him. He smiled at her.

"We'll take it," he said to Boogie's mother. "May I write you a check?"

And Betsy kissed Margaret, and hugged Louisa, and

said to Mrs. Hilton in a housewifely tone, "We'll eat our meals in front of this window sometimes."

The home Margaret had found for them was perfect, family and friends agreed—near a streetcar line so Joe could get to work conveniently, near the Ray house so Betsy could get back often, not too expensive, and not too big. That last was a factor for it must now be furnished.

They had discovered, in the Rays' basement, an old drop-leaf table. Mrs. Ray's father, when he came to Minnesota after the Civil War, had made it himself out of a black walnut tree. Mrs. Ray, who didn't like old-fashioned furniture, used it to hold the laundry basket. Joe and Betsy dragged it out in triumph.

In a secondhand store, Betsy and her mother found two small walnut chairs. They were just the period of the table and upholstered in rose damask. They found a big armchair for Joe, upholstered in blue.

In a new furniture store, they bought a handsome bookcase, and a blue and rose rug, and blue and rose draperies to hang at the sides of the triple-winged bay.

"No lace curtains! Nothing to hide my elm tree," Betsy insisted.

They bought a white-painted bedroom set, stenciled in blue and rose, and white ruffled bedroom curtains, and blue checked kitchen ones. All these treasures, along with a broom, dustpan, carpet sweeper, and shiny pots and pans! Betsy's desk came over from 909. And Mrs. Hawthorne gave Joe Saturday off, to settle.

"By afternoon," Betsy said at breakfast, "we'll be ready for callers. Why don't you be our first caller, Margaret, since you found us the apartment?"

"May I bring Boogie?" she asked eagerly.

"Of course."

"But don't come too early," Joe warned. "For after we get settled, we'll have to go out and stock up with groceries. And I mean stock up!"

"I've allowed ten dollars," Betsy said firmly.

Laden down with bags, and boxes full of wedding gifts, and a picnic lunch from Anna, Betsy and Joe went over to their apartment. Mrs. Hilton gave them the key. They went in, and closed the door, and hugged each other. Then Betsy tied an immaculate apron over an immaculate house dress, and Joe rolled up his sleeves.

They started by laying the blue and rose rug on the gleaming varnished floor. Next, they placed the bookcase against the right-hand wall, and settled their books. They wound the Hawthornes' clock and put it on top, in the center.

"Listen to it tick!" Betsy cried, as though no clock had ever ticked before.

On one side of the clock they put a dark blue vase that Joe's mother had treasured because Joe had bought it for her with money he had earned selling papers. On the other side they put a tall cup, striped in pink and blue and gold. It had been given to Betsy by a young baroness in Munich, and the poet Goethe was said to have drunk from it.

Opposite the bookcase, they placed the old-fashioned table, one leaf raised to lean against the wall. Betsy put more books on this, between book blocks, and a small pottery angel which had been made and given to her by the Christus of the Passion Play in Oberammergau.

She arranged the chairs, and Joe brought out a tape measure and a hammer which Mr. Ray had thoughtfully loaned, and hung the pictures where Betsy wanted them hung.

"Homekeeping Hearts are Happiest" and "The Hanging of the Crane" were spaced precisely to the left and the right of the clock, above the bookcase. Over the old walnut table went Lenbach's "Shepherd Boy." Margaret's three monkeys fitted into a niche beside the bay, and Joe's Harvard etchings hung in the foyer. They would make a dignified impression, Betsy said.

Van Dyke's "Flight Into Egypt" went into the bedroom, and a Japanese print of a long-legged bird in a marsh was hung above Betsy's desk. It had always hung there. For some mysterious reason, Betsy claimed, it made her feel like writing.

Everywhere were framed and unframed photographs of Betsy's family, Joe's father and mother, his uncle and aunt, their friends from high school and college. On the bureau stood Betsy in her high school graduating dress, and a snapshot of Joe which she had steamed out of a kodak book and carried through Europe.

The more they settled the apartment, the more

beautiful it looked. They beamed upon it, eating Anna's lunch in the bay window, and as soon as they had finished, they started working again.

"This is the last big job," Joe said, tackling the curtains. "As soon as I finish this, we'll go out and buy our groceries. I hope ten dollars buys a lot, Mrs. Hetty Green." He dropped a curtain rod to come over and kiss her. There was a ring at the back doorbell.

"That will be Margaret and Louisa. The idea," Betsy exclaimed as she ran, "of our first callers using the back door!"

Joe, returning to the curtain rod, did not follow until he heard a shriek.

Betsy was sitting on the kitchen floor beside a huge box overflowing with groceries. A smiling delivery boy was just closing the door.

"Who sent them?"

"He wouldn't say. But they're for us."

Joe dropped down beside her. He lifted out a dozen eggs, a half dozen tomatoes, a cucumber, some onions—two bottles of milk, a pound of butter, bacon, a slab of strong cheese—a loaf of bread, a coffee cake, doughnuts.

"Pretty good," he said, devouring one.

Betsy was pulling out coffee, cocoa and tea, vinegar and oil, salt and pepper, oatmeal, tapioca, molasses, raisins.

"And coconut!" she cried. "I can make you a coconut cake as soon as I learn how!"

Next came flour and sugar, baking powder, soda and vanilla. Beside a box of graham crackers stood a jar of jelly and one of pickles. Potatoes and apples spilled from their sacks.

"See here!" said Joe, presenting a large moist package on which someone had scrawled: "Joe is to broil this. Don't trust Betsy."

"It's Papa's writing."

"You have some father!"

"*We* have, you mean! Oh, I wish the phone was connected so we could call and thank . . ."

A doorbell was ringing again, the front one this time. And this time it was Margaret and Louisa.

They wore their new fall suits. They wore their hats, white gloves. Betsy wiped her hand on her skirt before she offered it in welcome. But they ignored her disheveled appearance. Their manners were as flawless as their attire.

Boogie presented a bouquet of chrysanthemums. "My mother sent them. She hopes you will be very happy here, and so do Bogie and I." Then she closed her lips, plainly resolved not to babble. Her rosy face took on an artificial smile.

"The apartment looks charming," said Margaret.

While Betsy ducked into the bathroom to wash, Joe hung their jackets in the closet off the foyer.

"We'll get calling cards when we graduate," Margaret remarked, glancing at the empty silver tray.

He showed them around the apartment with his best Harvard air, and they made small admiring sounds. When they reached the kitchen, with its dazzling display of groceries all over the floor, Louisa did give one squeal, but she put her hand over her mouth. Betsy passed her a doughnut.

"Isn't this just like Papa!" Margaret said in a fond superior tone.

Shortly she glanced at the watch Betsy had brought her from Europe. She glanced at Louisa. A first call, her look warned, only lasted fifteen minutes.

Louisa gulped her second doughnut. She sprang up and put on the artificial smile. She and Margaret shook hands with their hosts again and, with unimpaired dignity, departed.

Joe and Betsy leaned on the closed door, shaking with laughter.

Twilight was falling. Beyond their bay window, the gold of the elm tree was growing dim.

"I'm hungry as a curly wolf," said Joe. "And it takes you longer to dress than it does me. You may have the shower while I put away the groceries. And I'll broil the steak."

"I'll set the table," Betsy said. She wanted to make it beautiful for their first dinner.

Fresh from her bath, dressed in dark maroon silk and her sheerest apron, she opened the leaves of her Grandfather Warrington's table. She set it with a snowy cloth and napkins, and the silver with birds on the handles, and the china with pink and blue and lilac-colored flowers. She put white candles in the Hutchinsons' candlesticks, and Boogie's flowers in a vase.

Joe, resplendent now in white shirt and tie, was whistling as he broiled the steak. He shouted so many comments on his remarkable skill that Betsy came out to admire. He had set potatoes boiling, and she sliced a tomato and cucumber, and put bread and butter and jelly on the table. She made the coffee.

The steak was lifted to a hot platter, hissing. Betsy lit the candles, took off her apron, and sat down. Joe came in, holding the platter high, and at that moment a door bell rang a third time. They looked at each other in dismay.

"Oh, dear!" said Betsy. "Who could come calling at this hour?"

"On our first evening alone!" grumbled Joe. But he put down the platter and went to the door. Betsy followed.

It was Margaret, and she looked very different now. The hat was gone. So were the gloves. Her coronet braids had come loose, and one hung over her shoulder.

"Betsy!" she cried, but had to stop for breath. Her eyes were enormous. "They phoned us because your phone isn't connected."

"Who did?" Betsy asked. "What is it?"

"Easy now!" said Joe.

Margaret steadied herself against the door.

"Harry Kerr! About Tacy! She has a baby!"

"Oh! Oh!" Betsy fell upon Margaret with ecstatic hugs. "And Tacy's all right? And the baby? Does she have red hair?

Margaret's laughter was a soft, amused fountain.

"Betsy! Keep still, and let me finish telling you! You brought that doll from Germany for nothing! It's a boy!"

8

OF A MEAT PIE AND OTHER THINGS

"Mrs. Joseph Willard," read the new calling cards. Betsy looked at them with delight. She was very proud of being a wife, of Joe, of his extravagant devotion. She was radiantly happy in her new life.

It wasn't easy, though, to become a housekeeper.

Betsy had always joked about her lack of domestic

skills. She couldn't thread a needle, she was wont to announce blithely at sewing bees, and usually read aloud.

"Here, let me do that!" Joe or Cab or almost any boy in the Crowd would offer when Betsy started to make cocoa or scramble eggs.

"*Liebchen,*" Tib used to say, preparing a snack, "you sit down and watch. What you don't know about cooking would fill one of those books you plan to write."

It had been funny, but it wasn't funny now, with Joe coming home from work, smiling and hungry. He wanted something more for dinner than place mats and candlesticks. After kissing her fondly, he would go, sniffing, out into the kitchen.

"What's to eat?" he would ask.

That was a terrible moment!

Keeping the small apartment charming was not hard. It was a pleasure to wash the new dishes, to make the white bed with care, to dust the wedding presents and run the carpet sweeper up and down the living room, looking out into the elm and watching its leaves—as the days rolled by—turn from gold to brown, and fall, revealing a pattern of boughs which became, at last, narrow shelves for snow.

She did not do the heavy work. Joe had insisted on a weekly cleaning woman. Betsy had scoffed at the idea, quoting their split-penny budget.

So much for rent, so much for food and clothing, so much for telephone, gas and electricity, for the wet wash (she would do the ironing herself) and their personal allowances. A casual sum called incidentals was to cover the doctor, dentist, and amusements. Joe's insurance premiums must be paid. And they had resolved that ten dollars would go into their savings account every month if they had to live on corn meal mush.

"No!" Betsy had insisted. "No cleaning woman at two dollars a day!" And really, she explained earnestly, a child could keep their tiny apartment clean!

Joe, however, was adamant. And when Joe was adamant, Betsy soon discovered, he was even more adamant than she could be herself, although Betsy was famous for a will of iron. If her will was of iron, she thought now, there must be some undiscovered metal, even stronger, to describe Joe's will.

"I observed you, Mrs. Willard, on your honeymoon, and I feel sure you have never scrubbed a floor."

"I'm not too old to learn."

"I concede that it would be foolish for the average wife not to save two dollars weekly out of one hundred and fifty-five a month, by dispensing with outside help. But you're not the average wife."

"That's what every husband thinks."

"You want to be a writer. You want that more than anything else in the world."

"No," Betsy interrupted. Her voice was sober, "There's one thing I want more, Joe. I want to be a good wife to you—and a good mother to our children."

Joe patted her cheek. "We'll put it this way," he said. "You *are* a writer. You've always been writing stories, and the last few years you've been selling them."

"But except for that beautiful surprise when I got a hundred dollars from *Ainslee's*, I've never sold one for more than ten or twelve."

"Ten dollars," Joe replied triumphantly, "would pay your woman for five weeks."

She was stubbornly silent.

"It will be hard enough for you, honey," he ended, "just to learn to cook. You've promised to learn to make lemon pie and rice pudding. Remember?"

So Betsy juggled the budget and engaged a stout Marta to come every Friday, and soon she was very glad that Joe had overruled her. Learning to cook gave her plenty to do. Cooking was harder even than algebra had been.

She was thankful for her high school Domestic Science training, distant as that was. She still had the Dom. Sci. cookbook, but it was regrettably full of things like English monkey, banana and nut salad, and cream puffs.

She yearned to produce some of Anna's masterpieces, but when she asked about fried chicken:

"Why, lovey, you just put it into a skillet and fry it."

And about Lady Baltimore cake:

"I'll send one over to you tonight. Margaret can bring it."

Mrs. Ray's recipes called for too many eggs and too

much butter and whipping cream for the Willard budget. And she, also, was vague. Of her divine pie crust, she would say, twinkling her fingers, "You just put in lard till it feels right."

Betsy tried hard—with the pie crust and everything else. She did not forget the resolution she made on her wedding morning: *Learn to cook.* She did not forget the other resolutions, and was curled, powdered, perfumed, and wearing a pretty dress when Joe burst in after work. His face when he saw her was more than worth the trouble. But then would come that terrible question.

"What's to eat?"

One night when he went out to the kitchen, sniffing expectantly, the odor was acrid and smoky.

"What's wrong?" he asked.

"Nothing much," Betsy answered lightly. "I've made a meat pie and a little spilled and burned on the bottom of the oven."

"I love meat pie," said Joe, and went, whistling, to wash.

Betsy approached the oven dubiously. The accident had been a little more than "nothing much." She had thought she remembered just how Anna made meat pie—cutting leftover meat into chunks, and dropping it into gravy along with potatoes and onions and carrots, spreading biscuit dough on top. But something had gone wrong. The dough had overflowed and stuck to the floor of the oven, and burned. She had scraped it off, and scraped and scraped, but it kept on overflowing and sticking and burning and she had run frantically to fling up all the windows and run back to scrape some more. Eventually she had decided that the oven wasn't hot enough and had turned it up as high as it would go. Then the top of the depleted crust had burned.

Her meat pie didn't look like Anna's but she carried it bravely out to the dainty table.

Joe served it, and there was nothing else to serve, except sliced cucumbers. The value of a meat pie, she had been told, was that everything necessary to a nutritious meal could be included in it.

Joe took a bite. So did Betsy. Where the crust wasn't burned, it was soggy, and the vegetables tasted very queer. Joe took a second bite.

"A mighty good idea," he said briskly, "using up that pot roast in a meat pie. It's tasty, too."

Betsy put down her fork and tears came into her eyes.

"Why, honey!" Joe exclaimed. "What's the matter?"

Betsy began to cry. She pushed back her chair and ran out of the living room and threw herself across the white bed.

Joe followed. "What is it?" he asked anxiously. "Didn't I say your meat pie was good?"

"That's just the trouble!" Betsy sobbed. "It's so awful—and you were so—so—nice about it!"

At this Joe laughed his ringing laugh and kissed her tears away. "Next time I'll beat you."

"Next time," said Betsy, wiping her eyes fiercely, "it's going to be good! At least it's going to be fit to eat."

The following afternoon she went to see Tacy and the baby. She had seen the baby first in the hospital, and had been disappointed again. Kelly Kerr not only wasn't a girl—the next one would be, Tacy promised—but he wasn't at all pretty. He was red and had hardly a spear of hair. When Betsy started the soft admiring coos that people make over babies, Tacy had stopped her. She looked beautiful, sitting up in bed, her long red braids against the white pillow, but her eyes were a little anxious.

"Don't say he's handsome," she had said, "for I know better. He's going to develop a wonderful personality, though. That's what people do when they're not good looking, Harry says." And she cuddled the mite protectively.

The joke of it was that now he was getting pretty. He wasn't so red any more; light curls were sprouting; and he had Tacy's Irish eyes.

"I never saw such a change in a child!" Betsy cried, and Tacy let her hold him while she went out to the kitchen.

Over coffee and gingerbread, Betsy poured out the tale of the meat pie. Tacy was comforting, as always.

"Meat pie is hard," she said. "I still can't make a good one. I think, Betsy, you'd better stick to easier things for a while. Pork chops and baked potatoes. Meat loaf. Macaroni. Joe will like them just as well." She passed the gingerbread. "Learn to make this, before you try a Lady Baltimore cake."

It was good advice and was backed up shortly by a gift from Tib.

"This cookbook," she declared, presenting a business-like-looking volume, "tells all about everything. It practically says, 'take an egg and break it.' It's just right for people like you, Betsy, who otherwise might think the egg went in, shell and all."

Betsy burst into laughter. The practical gift was so in contrast to the appearance of the giver! Tiny, delicately formed, with a shower of golden curls, Tib seemed to have strayed out of a fairy tale. But cookbooks, Betsy well knew, were more in her line. She was highly proficient in all the domestic arts. When she came out to the Willards', she would find Betsy's mending basket and empty it while they talked. Or if it were near mealtime, she would tie on an apron.

She did that now, after taking off a feathered hat and the jacket of a pale green velvet suit. The skirt was draped to show a pleated underskirt.

"Pretty. *Nicht wahr?*" she asked. Tib often threw in German words, and her English had a little foreign twist. "I made it myself. It may not be just the thing for the office, but I dress as I please."

"It's simply darling! So original! But Tib, what heels! You need a husband to look after you!" said Betsy. "When are you going to settle down?"

"Settle down?" Tib gave an airy shrug. "Why should I settle down? I'm good at my job. Saving money. Like my boardinghouse. And one young man takes me to the dancing teas—all the hotels have them now—and another one takes me to everything good that comes to the Met."

"Like either of them?" asked Betsy cannily.

Tib got down a crockery bowl and the flour. She proposed to make dumplings for a lamb stew Betsy had on the fire. "They're *Lausbub'n*!" she replied. "That's what Grosspapa Hornik used to call the silly boys who kept phoning me in Milwaukee. Wanting to spend their money! Falling in love! And all because I have a few yellow hairs."

Betsy chuckled appreciatively.

"What does *Lausbub'n* mean?"

"Oh, good-for-nothing scalawags! It's slang. But they were all nice boys. Grossmama had to approve of them or I couldn't accept their invitations."

"How are your grandparents?" Betsy asked. She had visited Tib in Milwaukee and knew her relatives there. On the Muller side they were German, and rich. The Horniks, with whom Tib lived during her college years, were Bohemians from Austria. Grosspapa Hornik was a tailor.

"They're fine," Tib replied. "Of course they're upset about this dreadful war. So am I."

"Of course!" Betsy's voice was sympathetic. The war

must be hard on German-Americans like Tib who naturally would favor the Germans.

"The President asks us to be neutral," Tib went on.

"You try to be, I know."

Tib looked up in surprise. *"Lieber Gott,* I'm not neutral!"

"You're not?"

"Not by a jugful! And neither are my brothers!" She stirred vigorously. "Germany ought to get rid of that Kaiser. *Lausbube!"* she added scornfully.

Betsy burst into laughter again.

"I thought," she explained, "that you meant you weren't neutral because you favored the Germans."

"Ach, Betsy!" Tib replied. "Of course I love the German people. But you must remember that Grosspapa Hornik was a Forty-eighter."

"I know," answered Betsy. "He told me all about it. He came to this country in 1848 when he was a little boy. There had been a revolution in Austria, and his parents were in it, and they had to get out fast."

"Well," said Tib, "why do you think they objected to the old country? Too many uniforms! Too many wars! 'Kaisers are *nicht gut!'* Grosspapa is always saying. He mixes up German and English. But nobody loves America more than Grosspapa Hornik."

With a practiced hand she dropped spoonfuls of batter on top of the bubbling stew.

Betsy studied the cookbook Tib had brought. She

studied it with a concentration worthy of a profound scientific work. And following Tacy's suggestion, she mastered meat loaf. She learned to fry pork chops so they did not end up dry as chips, and to boil vegetables so they did not emerge waterlogged and soggy.

Doggedly she pushed on to lemon pie and rice pudding. The rice pudding his mother had made, Joe explained seriously, was a custard rice pudding, rich and yellow, with plenty of raisins in it.

"Betsy!" he exclaimed in delight as he ate. "You got it right!"

Tacy gave her a recipe for Never Fail pie crust. The filling was easy, and it was almost fun, Betsy admitted, to make a meringue. Certainly it was fun, when Joe came home, to escort him proudly to a golden brown pie.

He stared admiringly and cut a huge wedge.

"Joseph Willard! That's for dessert!"

He tasted it, rolled his eyes, kissed her solemnly on the brow.

"We are now," he declared, "officially man and wife."

"I'll call Dr. Atherton. He'll be so pleased!" said Betsy.

There were still plenty of failures, and on those nights Joe helped with the dishes. They were always in a hurry to get dishes done, for evenings were beautifully cozy. With shades drawn against the wintry night, Joe settled himself in the secondhand blue armchair, to read aloud. He was reading *Sentimental Tommy*. Sometimes

Betsy tried to darn, but darning, for her, was a major undertaking, and when she grew interested in the story she made mistakes.

Sometimes Joe would say, "Just be beautiful tonight!" And she would put on the pink negligee and let down her hair.

He talked about his work. The campaign had gone well. Minneapolis was digging deep for the Belgians, and Betsy was sure it was because of Joe's stories. He was another Richard Harding Davis, she said.

He had a problem, though. He was not sure he wanted to stay on with the Bureau. Mrs. Hawthorne's office, he told Betsy, was no place for him or any other man.

Mrs. Hawthorne brewed afternoon tea over a spirit lamp, sending one of the girl workers out for cakes. She took a great interest in their personal lives and was kept up to date on their beaus, their parties, their worries, and their clothes. Her warm rich laughter floated out over the office.

"She's brilliant. She's a whiz at her job. But I'll get soft if I stay."

"You'll be going on to the *Courier*," Betsy prophesied.

And that was exactly what happened.

"I can't afford to pay you what you're worth," Mrs. Hawthorne told him when the campaign ended. "But my husband has a place for you now."

To discuss this change, the Willards were invited to

the Hawthornes' for dinner. Betsy wore the dark maroon silk, dressed her hair with care, manicured her nails, added bracelets and perfume. Joe changed his tie twice, and they went out on the streetcar through a frigid December night.

The Hawthorne house stood on a corner. An arc light gleamed over the snowy lawn showing tall oak trees and a tall house with so many narrow gables that it seemed to rush up into points. Lights were pouring through the windows and a ringletted head peeked out of one.

Sally Day answered the door, wearing a reddish-brown velvet dress that matched her curls and eyes. Smiling elfishly, she drew them in and offered to play her new piano piece.

"Sally Day! Take their wraps!" Mrs. Hawthorne clapped reproving hands but the warm loving laugh Joe had described floated out over the hall.

Dinner was served by a maid in cap and apron. The atmosphere, however, was anything but formal. Mr. Hawthorne kept taking scraps of paper from his pockets, and reading aloud things he had liked and clipped or copied down. When he finished he would look around, eyes bright and eager behind his glasses.

He and Joe kept telling each other of books they ought to read, and Mr. Hawthorne kept jumping up to fetch books from the living room. At last he had a great stack beside his plate. He read aloud from Don Marquis, about archie and mehitabel, all through dessert.

Sally Day kept asking permission to play the new piece, and at last she, too, dashed into the living room, and played it. Returning to the table, she suggested that she dance.

"After a while, dear! Maybe Joe wants to walk on the ceiling."

Sally Day turned to Joe. "You can't!" she challenged.

After dinner, when Joe's transfer to the *Courier* was being discussed, Mrs. Hawthorne turned to Betsy.

"It will be hard for me to fill Joe's place," she said. "Would you like to try? I know you write. You might enjoy working in a publicity office."

Betsy was very pleased but her answer came promptly. "Oh, Mrs. Hawthorne, I know I'd love it! Joe has told me how delightful your office is. But, Mrs. Hawthorne, I already have a job."

"You have?" She sounded surprised.

"Yes. And it's important, and very hard. It's learning how to keep house."

Mrs. Hawthorne swept her arms around Betsy with laughter. "That's the girl!" she said.

9
A PLOT IS HATCHED

Before Joe began the new job, he and Betsy went to see Aunt Ruth. Betsy found it exciting to be a married woman visiting her husband's family—and Aunt Ruth was all the family Joe had. They were not related, really; her husband had been Joe's father's brother. But Joe had lived with them for several years after his mother's death when he was twelve.

Snow was packed along the flat streets of little Butternut Center. It was only a handful of houses, a church, and the general store, Willard's Emporium. Betsy had met Joe there, the summer before they started high school.

"You were eating an apple and reading a book the first time I saw you," she said. "Jinks, you were handsome!"

She had come again when they were eighteen and beginning to fall in love.

"That was when I met Uncle Alvin and Aunt Ruth and Homer." He was the clerk who now was helping Aunt Ruth run the store.

She lived above the store among fat chairs and sofas, all hung with old-fashioned tidies. The rooms were stuffily hot from a glowing pot-bellied stove. She was thin, gray-haired, with a kind, sad face. Betsy did not get very well acquainted with her, for Aunt Ruth and Joe were busy talking about people Betsy did not know.

Aunt Ruth cooked Joe's favorite dishes, and she wiped her eyes while he ate, saying how proud Uncle Alvin had been of him. "Your going through college and all!" She depended on him, too; asked his advice about the store. Joe listened thoughtfully.

"It sounds to me as though the store's pretty hard on you, Aunt Ruth. Homer wants to buy, you say. Why don't you sell?"

"Maybe I will," she answered. "I might go to California and get away from these cold winters. I have a niece out there."

But she always changed her mind.

"No," she would say, after a while. "I've lived in Butternut Center all my life. I was born here. And I think I'll stay on."

Christmas approached. The Willard apartment had a wreath in the snowy bay window. Mistletoe, tied to a small Santa Claus, swung in the doorway. There were hospitable dishes of candy and nuts about. There was even a small Christmas tree. But the heart of the holiday remained in the Ray house to which Joe and Betsy, laden with packages, tramped through a spectral Christmas Eve.

Joe had never seen a Ray Christmas before but he joined in with enthusiasm. After carols and reading beside a tree that glittered to the ceiling, Mr. Ray turned out the lights and everyone scrambled about, filling the socks and stockings that hung around the fire. In the morning, between grabs at a buffet breakfast, they pulled out their presents in uproarious gaiety.

Joe gave Betsy a cameo brooch. She pinned it ecstatically into the cherry-red bathrobe while Kismet lunged through tissue paper after catnip and Mr. Ray paraded with a cane his wife had given him.

"Now swing it like Joe does!" she commanded, and Mr. Ray marched up and down, eating a sausage and imitating Joe's swagger way with a cane.

Canes were not so common in Minneapolis as they had been in Boston. Only Jimmy Cliff, among Joe's fellow workers on the *Courier,* carried one. Joe described this young man delightedly. A reporter, he was also a poet—hugely stout, wearing loose easy clothes, a slouch hat, and a Windsor tie.

"A wonderful kid who'll never grow up. He's married, and wants us to come out to their house and talk writing."

Meeting Jimmy Cliff was one of the few pleasant experiences Joe had had since returning to the *Courier.* He had been assigned to the courthouse—not a bad run, he said—but he had found trouble there.

Joe told Betsy about it cheerfully at first. The two rival reporters were older, and cronies. They made the rounds of the courthouse offices together, and had not suggested that he join them.

"In fact, they froze me out."

Joe had not minded making the rounds alone, but he had found news sources equally difficult, especially one bearded official who was the political bellwether of the building.

"I don't know what the old fellow has against me."

"What *could* he have against you?" It was inconceivable to Betsy that anyone should dislike Joe.

"Plenty, evidently! He never gives me any news that isn't already public property."

In a few days an important courthouse story appeared on the front page of the two other newspapers. It was missing from the *Courier.* Joe was humiliated and ashamed.

"Hawthorne chewed me up," he said.

"That nice Mr. Hawthorne?" Betsy cried in indignant astonishment.

"Friendship doesn't hold him back when the paper is scooped, and it darn well shouldn't!"

After this incident, Joe stopped talking about his work, and he cut Betsy short if she brought up the subject. She started to read all three newspapers, and one day she found that the *Courier* had missed another big courthouse story. It happened a third time.

Joe started coming home late, looking grim. He was almost always in the mood of intense concentration he had shown the day he was hunting for a job. Betsy knew he was trying desperately to solve his problem. She tiptoed about, trying not to disturb him.

One evening, in spite of herself, she chuckled out loud. She was reading a feature story on the front page of the *Courier*. It was only a paragraph long, but very funny—about a will that concerned seven Siamese cats. Joe looked up darkly, and she hastily grew sober.

But the next night she chuckled again, over a similar brief story about a suit filed by a party-goer who had been brought low by a two-inch *femme fatale*—his host's daughter's dolly.

"Who's writing these?" She looked at Joe suspiciously. "They sound like you."

"I'm writing 'em," Joe said, but so glumly that she did not say more. She kept looking for the little features, though, and they kept on appearing, and a night came when Joe burst into the apartment, grinning from ear to ear. He handed her the *Courier,* and the biggest story on page one was a courthouse story signed by Joseph Willard.

"Darling!" Betsy hugged him, and he hugged her until she pulled away to sit down and read. "But how did you get it?"

He began to talk excitedly. "I was sunk. I couldn't get any news, and Hawthorne kept chewing me up. So, trying to make up for the stories I was missing, I started spending hours in the document room. The other boys never go in there. It's just a morgue for papers."

"What kind of papers?"

"Oh, papers filed by citizens having court troubles—complaints, countercomplaints, bills of particulars, suits for damages. You have to dig to find one with a story in it. And even when you've found one"—Joe looked mischievous—"you have to know how to put in the twist that makes it funny, or tragic, or heart-warming."

"You have to write like Joe Willard!" said Betsy. "But you found those features there!"

"Yes, and Hawthorne played them up. And today came the pay-off. The other boys approached me, sweet as pie. The reason I hadn't been getting all the news, they said, was that the old bellwether didn't like me. He felt the paper had insulted his dignity by sending a kid to the courthouse. He didn't like my way with words. He didn't like my cane.

" 'But he isn't a bad sort,' the boys said. 'You start making the rounds with us. When he sees you're one of the gang, he'll come around.' And he did." Joe thumped the paper. "He not only gave me this story—he started kidding me about my cane!"

"But those miserable reporters!" cried Betsy. "What brought about their change of heart?"

"Why, their city editors were chewing *them* up because they were missing the stories I'd dug out of the document room. Those boys are swell, really, Betsy. They just hadn't seen any reason why they should drop in my lap news sources they'd spent years developing. But they see now, and they've smoothed things out for me, and naturally they've suggested that when I find a good story I might just tell them which document to look at."

"And will you?"

"Of course."

Betsy bounced. "A lot of good it will do them! *They* can't write like Joe Willard! Oh, Joe, I'm so happy!"

She was very happy—because of his triumph, and because his low mood was gone. But although things went smoothly on the *Courier* after that, Joe's low moods came back sometimes.

Betsy had known, of course, that he had low moods, just as he had high ones, but she had not known the low ones reached such subterranean depths. For a time they made her deeply anxious. Was she to blame? Did he regret his marriage? Not love her any more? But she knew that wasn't true.

Joe, she came to realize, had a complex temperament, quite different from her own which was simple and easily understood. He had boundless courage. In a bad situation he always fought back. But he worried to a degree incomprehensible to Betsy.

He had told her he worried about money. That was why he wanted her to manage the budget. She found out now that he worried about his work, about his contacts with people.

It's astonishing, when he's so wonderful, she thought, trying with might and main to understand.

Perhaps his imagination was too vivid? He could invent too many possible bad happenings. Or perhaps being orphaned so young—those years of loneliness—had been harder on him than he knew?

When he was feeling gloomy he did not want to be praised or encouraged. He wanted to be let alone. All she could do, she decided, was what she did instinctively—show him always that she loved him and admired him and was proud of him.

And so she adjusted herself to Joe's low moods.

"He's probably adjusting himself to plenty of things about me. My cooking, for example."

That was improving, and so was her ironing. At first, she felt sure, Joe had not dared to take off his coat in the office. But now she could manage those awkward collars and cuffs. She had almost stopped scorching. And as housework grew less demanding, she had more time for other things, especially—being Betsy—her writing.

It was good for her writing to be alone all day in the quiet apartment. Sometimes there were frost patterns on the windows, strange scenes that had never been created before and would never be created again. Sometimes a fierce, brilliant bluejay perched on their elm. After a snowfall blankets of white covered the boughs, the lawns, the rooftops. It was all clarity and purity, up and down Bow Street.

Betsy would stand looking out the window. Then she would get a tablet and some pencils and start a story.

In the evenings Joe read her stories and made suggestions for improving them. "Silver Hat" paid Marta for a month. Joe made up a plot, and Betsy wrote the story, and he rewrote it. "Mr. Forrester Leaves for Tibet," signed by both of them, paid Marta for six weeks more. Joe started another. Betsy couldn't help with that one; it was about a prize fight and she couldn't understand it. But "The Uppercut" paid Marta twelve weeks into the future.

Joe and Betsy began to dream great dreams.

The dreams filled many evenings, which was well. If the budget was to operate—and it did, with the help of corn meal mush now and then—they could not go, as the Hutchinsons did, to the Symphony Orchestra concerts or, like Tib and her beaus, to the plays that came to the Metropolitan. They went to the stock company, sometimes, on passes picked up at the *Courier*, and to the movies to see long-curled Mary Pickford and that funny, sad man, Charlie Chaplin. But for the most part their lives were quiet, and Betsy was pleased when Tib called one morning and asked her downtown for lunch.

"There's a cute new place. You telephone your order from the table."

Betsy enjoyed dressing up in her Paris suit and hat, her high pearl-buttoned shoes and heavy coat. She took the streetcar downtown, and Nicollet Avenue was crowded, shop windows were exciting, and the new restaurant was gay.

Betsy arrived first, and heads turned when Tib came in, walking haughtily on her high heels. Perhaps because she was so diminutive, Tib affected a disdainful air. It was confusing, like so many things about her, for she was the soul of good nature.

Her dark coat sprang out below her tiny waist in fur-edged tiers. A fur cap sat on her sunrise hair.

"Mrs. Vernon Castle in person!" Betsy cried, for that goddess of the dance affected caps.

Tib gave her tickled little laugh. "Well," she answered factually, "I'm going dancing after the store closes."

"One of the *Lausbub'n*?"

"No, Fred."

Her brother Fred was studying architecture at the University. A slender, fair-haired young man, he danced as beautifully as his sister did and often took her to his fraternity parties or a *Thé Dansant*.

When Tib had efficiently telephoned their order, Betsy asked, "What happened to the *Lausbub'n*?"

Tib gave her airy shrug. "Oh, they always find out that I'm not what they think I am. I could tell them in the first place. In fact, I try to. I'm not a flirt. The trouble is they never believe me."

Betsy began to laugh, but Tib spoke seriously. "Every man has a secret notion that he's going to marry a blonde. And when he sees me, he thinks I'm it. But I'm not!"

"You're a blonde."

"But not the kind of blonde I look like. For example, they think I live on rose petals." And she raised delicate eyebrows at the corned beef and cabbage the waitress had just placed before her.

"Oh, Tib! Tib!" laughed Betsy.

"They think I'm frivolous," Tib went on, "because I have so many pretty clothes. But you know I make most of them myself. Often I rip a dress up at night and it comes to the store a different one next day."

"I know."

"But that's not the worst of it." She put down her fork. "Just because I'm small, men think I'm a clinging vine. They think I need to be protected. Imagine that! Why, I like to paddle my own canoe! I like adventure. I want to see the world."

She was so much in earnest that Betsy stopped laughing. "Don't be so hard on them, honey! You *are* deceiving! Take the war—"

Most people didn't think much about that any more. Since the opposing armies had settled down for the winter in so-called trenches, the war wasn't so interesting as it had been at first. Betsy grieved about it sometimes. But she was so happy that she tried to put it out of her mind. Tib was different.

"You're so much more concerned about the war than anyone would expect you to be," Betsy tried to explain.

"*Ja*, that's another thing! I'm serious. I read the newspapers. But these men think I'm a *Dummkopf*. Don't bother your little yellow head about the war, they say! Think about me, instead! *Lausbub'n!*"

Tib turned to apple pie à la mode. "I'm saving my money to buy an automobile," she remarked in her usual cheerful tone.

"An automobile!" Betsy did not know an unmarried girl who owned an automobile. They were still not common. Old Mag, the Ray horse, had not liked Minneapolis and had long since been sent to the peaceful countryside. But Mr. Ray had not bought an automobile.

"No one in our family even knows how to drive," Betsy said.

"Well, I do!" answered Tib. "I used to drive my Uncle Rudy's auto. When I've bought my own, I'm going to go traveling."

"In the *auto*?"

"In the auto."

"But the roads! You'd get stuck! And who'd change your tires?"

"I would."

"Or some man who thinks he's going to marry a blonde."

Betsy burst into laughter again, and this time Tib joined her. Tib was sometimes a little slow to see a joke. But when she understood, she responded with delight. Her appreciation of other people's wit was one of her most endearing traits.

"*Ja*, that's good! Let them change my tires, the *Lausbub'n*! I'm going to drive my auto all over the United States."

If she keeps on talking like that, Betsy thought, Tacy and I will never be bridesmaids. And the next day she telephoned Tacy and asked her to bring the baby and come over, to discuss something important.

Tacy came in, her color even richer than usual from the cold. Kelly's cheeks were like winter roses. Tacy took off his bonnet and proudly fluffed up his light hair. It was perceptibly thick and curly now.

"What a chunk of sweetness!" Betsy cried, hugging him.

"Isn't he a cherub?"

When Betsy had brought in coffee and muffins— muffins were her latest accomplishment—she reported Tib's plans.

"She isn't even thinking about getting married!" Betsy cried. "She goes out all the time but she doesn't give a snap for the men."

"When girls don't marry young," Tacy said profoundly, "they get fussier all the time."

"That's right. You know the old saying about a girl going through the forest and throwing away all the straight sticks only to pick up a crooked one in the end." Betsy looked wise as befitted an old married woman.

"There's a lot of truth in that."

"And Tib will soon be earning so much money that she won't meet many men who earn as much money as she does."

"That would be bad."

"And then she'll start driving around in her car, and getting more and more independent, and she won't marry at all, maybe! And then what will she do when she's old?"

Betsy and Tacy looked at each other in alarm.

"She can come and play with my children," said tender Tacy. Although Kelly was sleeping, she picked him up and hugged him.

"Of course," volunteered Betsy, "she can have a share in Bettina. Whenever I *get* Bettina! But the best thing, Tacy, is for you and me to get busy and find the right one for her. Ask Harry to think about it. Joe's friends are all newspaper men, and they're very interesting, but they're *not* rich, and you know Tib! She's so practical.

She'd be more apt to marry someone with money."

"Harry can find someone," Tacy said confidently.

Tacy thought Harry could do anything. Betsy thought Joe could do anything. But with the perfect accord which had always characterized their friendship, they agreed that both husbands were supermen and never made comparisons.

Kelly had been wakened by the hug, and Tacy discovered that it was time to go. But while Betsy made macaroni and cheese—a good winter meal, and cheap, too—she kept thinking about their plan.

She told Joe about it at dinner, but he didn't take it seriously.

"You women! I should think anyone as pretty as Tib could do her own matchmaking!"

Before Betsy had time to reply, the telephone rang, and it was Tacy, her voice quivering with excitement.

"Betsy!"

"Yes."

"You know what we were planning—about Tib?"

"Yes, yes!"

"Well, Harry has just the one. He's a New York millionaire!"

"A millionaire!"

"Well, practically!"

Betsy squealed until the small apartment echoed. Joe came rushing to share the receiver.

"Can you and Joe come to dinner Saturday night? If I

can get Tib, that is! Harry has already called this Mr. Bagshaw."

"Yes, yes, we'll come! Oh, Joe! Isn't it thrilling?"

But Joe, after discovering the nature of the news, had gone back to his macaroni. It was good.

10
A MILLIONAIRE FOR TIB

"Bagshaw!" said Joe. "Bags of money—p'shaw!" And he was so pleased with his joke that he took Betsy for a running slide along the frozen sidewalk. "Wait till I tell that to Harry and Sam!"

"Joe Willard!" Betsy panted, "Don't you dare!"

"Lady, I dare anything!" Chuckling wickedly, he hurried her along under the icy stars and into the sizzling lobby of the Kerrs' apartment building.

Harry greeted them, holding a sturdy angel in a white flannel nightgown, embroidered in blue, who inspected them brightly while scraping a rattle across his father's well-brushed hair.

"Here! Stop that!" Harry said. "I'm putting him to bed, Joe. Want to help? I'm sure our Little Aids to Cupid need to talk over their big enterprise."

Joe threw an arm around his friend's shoulders. He hissed, "Bags of money—p'shaw!"

"You two behave yourselves!" Betsy ordered as they whooped, and she ran into the bedroom to drop her wraps, pat her hair, and smooth down the dark maroon silk.

The roomy apartment was even more immaculate than usual—and Tacy was always a meticulous housekeeper; Betsy never ceased to marvel at it. There were daffodils and pussywillows on the living room table. The dining room waited in formal splendor.

"Hello!" Tacy called from the kitchen. She was kneeling at the oven, gingerly drawing out a roasting pan. She lifted it to the top of the stove, and transferred a plump, savory bird to a hot platter.

"Roast chicken," she remarked, covering it snugly, "and chocolate meringue pie are my company dinner. It's a great help, Betsy, to have one company dinner that you know how to make really well."

With the assurance born of practice, she set about compounding giblet gravy.

"When I can make gravy for a millionaire," Betsy said, "I'll think I have arrived." She perched on a kitchen stool. "Tell me about our hero."

Tacy laughed and stirred. "Well, he's a widower! Older than Harry! Out here for an eastern bank. He's trying to get the bank's money out of a bankrupt wholesale dry goods house. He'll be in town several months, Harry says."

"How marvelous!"

"He's a friend of Harry's boss. Mr. Goodrich is in Florida and asked Harry to meet Mr. Bagshaw's train and help him get settled. He's staying at the Club."

"The Club! It sounds like an English novel."

"He plays bridge with a group there. He knows all the Minnesota bigwigs, including Sam's father. And he's taken a great liking to Harry. He *hinted* that he'd like to come out here. He hinted it the very day you and I were talking about Tib."

"It's Fate!" Betsy cried, jumping up, and the doorbell rang and Tacy stripped off her apron, revealing dark green elegance, but she put the apron on again, for the new arrivals were only Carney and Sam.

Sam joined the men in Kelly's room and Carney, looking as pretty as a pink, came out to the kitchen, borrowed an apron, and started to mash the potatoes. Tacy was stirring up baking powder biscuits now. Betsy was allowed to make ice water.

"But don't fill the glasses yet. Tib will be a little late."

"We planned it that way," Betsy explained.

"Does she know about this scheme?" asked Carney.

"Heavens, no! We're acting very casual."

"She asked if she shouldn't bring a man."

Carney snorted. "You two always did dream up fantastic things!"

"I don't see what's fantastic about Tib marrying a millionaire!" said Betsy, righteously indignant.

"Tib won't be a bit flustered by a million dollars," Tacy said.

"She'll be as cool as a cucumber in a Fifth Avenue mansion," said Betsy. "Brownstone fronts! I've seen 'em!"

"But it's so ridiculous! You marry someone you fall in love with."

"Well, how can Tib fall in love with this Mr. Bagshaw until she meets him?"

Carney was stumped by that. The doorbell rang again and this time Tacy and Carney both pulled off their aprons, and Tacy joined Harry at the door.

Mr. Bagshaw was tallish, thin, with a small dark mustache and dark hair carefully arranged to hide a bald spot! He wore convex eyeglasses which gave him an inscrutable look. He seemed able to see them better than they saw each other. And he was, Betsy admitted with a shock, definitely older even than Harry, who topped the rest by a few years.

"He must be nearly forty."

But he had the fascination of this great maturity. Suave, leisurely, he passed a leather cigarette case, selected a cigarette, and poised it in long, slender fingers, inquiring about Sam's father. Betsy followed Tacy to the kitchen.

"Isn't he perfect?" she whispered.

Tacy's eyes sparkled. "Speaking of English novels! He'll expect the men to stay behind after dinner with port and cigars."

"If he were spending the night, he'd put out his boots!"

Tacy popped the biscuits into the oven and she and Betsy dashed back to the living room, for the bell was ringing again.

Betsy heard Tib's light, gay voice saying good-by to a male voice on the threshold. Then she came in, waving her muff.

"Wie gehts?" she cried and ran to kiss Betsy and Carney, and threw elfin kisses to Joe, Harry, and Sam. When Mr. Bagshaw was presented, however, the affectionate little Tib vanished.

"How do you do?" she asked, putting on her disdainful air.

When she acts like that, Betsy thought, she's like a little girl playing lady.

Tib drew Betsy to the bedroom where she doffed her fur cap and fur-trimmed coat. Betsy expected a question about Mr. Bagshaw, but Tib only wanted to show off her dress—lavender messaline with a short tunic wired out above a slinky skirt.

"I finished it after work tonight," she said, pirouetting.

She took down her yellow hair and dressed it again in the feathery swirl which was Tib's version of the French roll. She liked this style because it made her look taller, and put in a shell pin which added another inch.

Back in the living room, the boys began to tease her while Mr. Bagshaw took off his glasses, polished them with a snowy handkerchief and put them back, looking at Tib all the while.

"How's the big business woman?"

"What dance have you learned today?"

"And what dance did you learn yesterday?"

"The lulu-fado. And if you weren't such clodhoppers, I'd show you how to do it."

Mr. Bagshaw spoke softly. "They were dancing the lulu-fado when I left New York."

Tib raised her eyebrows. "Do you dance it?"

"I attempt it," he replied in polite deprecation.

"After dinner," she said loftily, "if we can find the right record, I'll see how you do it." She turned to Tacy. "May I make the gravy, darling?"

"All made. Everything's ready." Tacy acted calm, but her cheeks were like flames.

At dinner the talk continued to be youthfully lively.

Mr. Bagshaw did more listening than talking, and more looking than either. He looked at Tib. Now and then polishing his glasses, now and then poising a cigarette in long, nervous fingers, he watched her intently. Tib had forgotten him and was laughing and chattering, enjoying the ease of being with old friends.

The company dinner was perfection.

I must learn a company dinner, Betsy thought as Harry carved second portions and the gravy, steaming hot, was passed again.

Mr. Bagshaw, although he ate sparingly, accepted a second biscuit with high praise.

"See what I mean, Rick?" asked Harry. He always found it easy to get on a first-name basis.

Carney decided to help out the plot. "You ought to taste Tib's cooking," she observed.

Mr. Bagshaw smiled at Tib. "What does she specialize in? Rose petals?" he asked, and Tib gave Betsy a look.

Oh, dear! How unfortunate! Betsy thought.

But when they finished the chocolate meringue pie and coffee, and gathered in the living room again, Mr. Bagshaw redeemed himself. He not only talked, he took command of the conversation and was most interesting.

He had been present at the sensational New York opening, two or three weeks before, of a motion picture called *The Birth of a Nation*.

"It was stupendous!" he said.

He spoke of *The Ziegfeld Follies* and *The Passing Show*—of Rector's, where one dined and danced in a grove of palms.

"I plan to go to New York some day," said Tib in a patronizing tone.

He had seen Mr. and Mrs. Vernon Castle and discussed their effect on the dance craze. They had not returned, he said, to the old forms; they used the new rhythms, but with grace and elegance.

"They've brought us out of the turkey-trot–bunny-hug vulgarity. The maxixe and the tango are quite lovely."

"That's true," Tib said, looking at him with respect.

Sam, returning from a trip outside to warm up the engine of his car, suggested bridge, but Harry demurred.

"Rick wouldn't like our bridge, woman bridge and no stakes."

"I'm sure it would be delightful," Mr. Bagshaw said. "But how about that lulu-fado Miss Muller was kind enough to suggest?"

"Yes," said Tib. "What records do you have, Tacy?" And she and Mr. Bagshaw strolled out to the glassed-in porch where the phonograph stood. Betsy and Tacy exchanged meaningful glances.

Evidently the Kerrs did not have the proper record for a lulu-fado.

"We'll have to go to the Radisson and dance it," Betsy heard Mr. Bagshaw say.

They began a maxixe.

Tib's dancing was lighter than foam, lighter than a hummingbird, lighter than a flower in a breeze. And Mr. Bagshaw was dexterous in the turns and dips and tricky skating steps. He danced very well, despite his age, Betsy noted with relief. The plot would have collapsed if he hadn't.

They put on a fox-trot, and everyone started dancing.

By the sea, by the sea,
By the beautiful sea . . .

Betsy whirled in Joe's arms.

"You're the prettiest girl at the party," he whispered.

They put on "Tipperary," but then in the midst of all the gaiety something pressed on Betsy's heart. For she had seen the British Territorials march off to war to that tune, just boys most of them, and many had not come back. Crossing battle lines, she thought of her dear German servant, Hanni, who had so wished to come to America, and of the Baroness Helena who had given her the cup that Goethe drank from!

Betsy was glad when "Tipperary" ended. (The next record was "I Didn't Raise My Boy To Be a Soldier.") Soon everyone stopped dancing except Tib and Mr. Bagshaw, who executed a tango. As they finished that, his voice floated into the living room.

"You don't look like Mrs. Castle. She looks like a boy, and you look like a sprite. But you dance with the same impersonal grace."

Betsy leaned toward Tacy. "Even Tib can't resist that!" she whispered.

When the party broke up, Sam called out that he would drive everyone home. Joe and Betsy accepted with thankful shivers, but Tib refused carelessly.

"Thanks a lot. Rick's taking me," she said.

Rick! Betsy and Tacy telegraphed that to Carney.

"Boy!" said Sam. "I didn't know you had a car here, or I'd have warned you. You have to go out and warm up the engine once in a while, in this Minnesota weather."

"Oh, my chauffeur is picking me up!" Mr. Bagshaw glanced surprisingly at his wrist. He was the first man Betsy had ever seen wear a watch on his wrist. "He's out there now."

Tib did not flick an eyelash.

They all heaped Tacy with compliments, and Mr. Bagshaw took her hand.

"The Club chef could not duplicate that dinner, Mrs. Kerr. But may I duplicate the guests? Can't you all dine with me a week from tonight?"

He turned to Tib, but she reverted in a flash to her disdainful air.

"Really, Rick!" she protested. "I can't make an engagement without my book. I do know, though, that I'm busy for the next two Saturday nights."

Mr. Bagshaw seemed amused, but respectfully so. He restrained a smile. "Then we'll make plans after Miss Tib has consulted that overstuffed engagement book. I do hope we can find an evening when all of you are free."

Next morning early Betsy and Tacy were on the telephone. Mr. Bagshaw, they agreed triumphantly, had fallen. Now the vital issue was Tib's reaction. Had she liked him, and how well?

"She seemed impressed."

"But did you notice how she crushed him when he tried to make a date?"

"Oh, that was just technique! No girl gives a man the first date he asks for."

"I hope you're right." Tacy was a little doubtful. "Well, we can talk it over tonight. Harry and I are going to 909 for Sunday night lunch."

"Oh, good!" Betsy exclaimed, for she was longing to turn the subject inside out, and Joe was already bored with it.

"Tib will never marry that grand-daddy!" he said.

"Joe, he's only a little older than Harry, and perfectly fascinating!"

"So are you—fascinating, that is."

"Don't you like him?"

Joe grinned. "Well, it was entertaining to see the colonel unbend to the privates for the sake of a pretty girl."

He was more interested in the pancakes he was tossing than he was in getting Tib married. "Did you ever see more beautiful pancakes? Butter this stack, Betsy, while I fry some more."

He and Betsy both loved Sunday, when they were together all day long. One thing troubled her a little. She
had almost stopped going to church. Joe had gone very
seldom since leaving Butternut Center, and now
although he went with Betsy when she asked him to,
he seemed to feel that the proper Sunday routine was
to sleep late and make pancakes for breakfast. Betsy
ate them in pink negligee and cap. Then she had an
extra good dinner to get, and Joe liked to read the Sunday papers, and they fed the squirrels that came to their
snowy window ledge. This morning a robin appeared in
the elm—fat, bright, and undismayed by the still arctic
cold.

"After all, it *is* March!" Betsy pointed out that afternoon when she and Joe walked down to the lake to
watch the skaters. "Tacy and I could find crocuses up on
the Big Hill, if we were back in Deep Valley."

They ended the walk at the Ray house where Sunday
night lunches were a family tradition. Mr. Ray always
made sandwiches. There was a crackling fire, and friends
of all ages dropped in. It made Betsy feel very much married to see Margaret playing the piano while her high
school friends sang.

Margaret had not acquired a real Crowd such as
Betsy had had in high school. But Louisa was always
there, and sometimes a boy or two. Betsy asked her
mother how Margaret got on with boys.

"They admire her," Mrs. Ray said thoughtfully.

"They take her to school parties. But they're a little scared of her, I think. You know how dignified she is, and she does nothing to encourage them."

"How about Louisa?"

"She and Margaret help each other. Margaret helps to tone her down, and she draws Margaret out of her shell."

After the Kerrs arrived, they talked about last night's party. Mrs. Ray was in on the plot.

"Three Little Aids to Cupid!" Harry chortled, and the men withdrew to discuss the Great War, as it was beginning to be called. Spring, everyone believed, would bring a big British offensive which might end the conflict.

Mrs. Ray, Betsy, and Tacy aired their great topic like a blanket suspected of moths.

"Have you heard from Tib today?" Mrs. Ray asked.

"No, and whenever we do, we must be sure to act casual."

"If we didn't, we'd antagonize her, Mrs. Ray."

"You should have heard her, Mamma, when he tried to make a date for next Saturday night!"

"I wish she'd phone," Mrs. Ray said.

"She won't. She won't think he's important enough. You know Tib!"

But the telephone shrilled through this prophecy, and the war, and Margaret's friends' singing. And it was Tib!

"I knew where to find you, *Liebchen*," she laughed.

"I'm sorry to interrupt those onion sandwiches, but Rick has telephoned twice. He does want to get that party at the Club arranged. I told him I'd check with you and Tacy."

Betsy stiffened in her effort to keep calm.

"Tacy's here," she said offhandedly.

"Then how about a week from Friday night?"

"Hold the line!"

Betsy and Tacy conferred in hushed jubilation.

"All right with everyone," Betsy reported brightly. "What do you think? I saw a robin today."

Tib lowered her voice. "Betsy," she said, "I have something else to tell you."

"What is it, dear?" Betsy's voice was gentle, but she signaled wildly to Tacy who rushed up on tiptoe, Mrs. Ray following.

"*So soon?*" she whispered. Betsy put a finger to her lips.

"Something perfectly marvelous," Tib went on. "It's the most marvelous thing that ever happened to me."

Betsy rounded her eyes at Tacy and shook an elated hand in the air. "Tell me about it, honey."

"Well, you know Rick took me home!"

"Yes." Still rounder eyes, a more elated hand.

"Well, that car—it's just one he's been renting! He's having his own car sent from New York. And, Betsy, what do you think?"

"About what?"

"About the car, of course!" Tib sounded impatient, for Betsy's tone was suddenly flat. "He's going to let me drive it. Think of that! I'm going to practically have my own car, all summer long."

11
NO TROUBLES TO PACK

Pack up your troubles in your old kit bag,
And smile, smile, smile . . .
The crowd of old friends, and Mr. Bagshaw, had no
troubles to pack, but to that tune they danced away the
summer.

Of course, "Pack Up Your Troubles" was a war song,

but a new one, and the war was a fire burning very far away. Twice in the spring its glare reached them briefly. When a strange new horror called poison gas was used by the Germans, Americans saw that glare. They were shocked because Canadian troops were stricken; Canada was close to home. And when a U-boat sank the British liner, *Lusitania*, one hundred and fourteen Americans were drowned.

That night Joe came home late, looking tired and sober, but excited, too. He took Betsy slowly into his arms.

"We'll be in it now," he said and she felt cold fingers on her heart. But President Wilson announced there was such a thing as being "too proud to fight," and although Joe and Mr. Ray and many others, including Colonel Roosevelt, objected to that view, it seemed to cool the country's wrathful fever. No big offensive came. Everything quieted down. And through that carefree summer of 1915, young and old continued to dance.

Certainly the Crowd danced—in smart hotels as Mr. Bagshaw's guests, in their homes entertaining Mr. Bagshaw, and, when the weather turned hot, at country clubs and leafy lakeside places Mr. Bagshaw was aware of. They danced the merry one-step and the swaying, gliding tango and the maxixe and the hesitation.

Mr. Bagshaw delighted in leading Tib out to the dance floor, a blonde sprite in a gossamer dancing cap and filmy dress, the jeweled ribbons of tango slippers tied about her dainty ankles.

Ankles could be seen, for skirts were getting shorter. Girls were standing straighter. The debutante slouch was gone. Minneapolis quoted, chuckling, from its popular columnist, "Q":

> *The joyful news is with us,*
> *Let paeans now be sung.*
> *The girls again have vertebrae*
> *On which their forms are strung.*
> *No longer does a figure S*
> *Come slouching down the street,*
> *The girls have got their backbones back,*
> *Instead of in their feet.*

"I'd like to meet that 'Q,'" Betsy said. "Why don't you ask him out some night?"

"Him!" laughed Joe. "It's a girl. A very nice, demure one. She and Jimmy Cliff are always swapping rhymes."

There were Expositions going on in California. Mr. Ray took Mrs. Ray and Margaret to see them. They would visit Mrs. Ray's mother, too. Anna took Kismet and the goldfish bowl to the country. Betsy missed them all, but being so entirely on her own made her feel even more married than usual, and that feeling was sweet.

Louisa, lonely for Margaret, dropped in with bouquets from the garden. The elm tree now was thickly, darkly green. But all the secrets of its branches were revealed to the Willard bay window. Running her carpet sweeper blithely up and down, Betsy watched a robin's nest, the eggs, the fledglings.

"I think I'll write a story about a little girl going to live with the birds!"

It was hot and she did her housework early, then closed the windows and drew the shades as she had seen her mother do. When Joe came in from work, he remarked with satisfaction that their apartment was the coolest spot in town.

Usually they were off for a swim or a sail or a picnic. Mr. Bagshaw dodged the picnics. But the Willards and the Kerrs met often at Lake Harriet's picnic grounds, adjoining the pavilion where band concerts were played.

"A Betsy-Tacy picnic!" Betsy and Tacy would say, spreading the table.

It wasn't exactly a Betsy-Tacy picnic. There was much more food than they had ever carried up the Big Hill. With husbands to feed, they brought salads, cold meats, pots of beans, layer cakes, and thermos bottles full of coffee. Kelly would be put down to crawl. He crawled very young, Harry and Tacy pointed out, watching the curly head progress in determined jerks across the grass.

Clearing the table, Betsy and Tacy would discuss Tib and Mr. Bagshaw. He wanted them to call him Rick and they managed to when he was around, but when he wasn't they still used the respectful "Mr. Bagshaw."

Tacy was able to report on him because Harry saw him every day. On Tib, Betsy was better informed. She and Joe were frequent companions of the romantic couple on weekends when the Kerrs were at the lake.

"Mr. Bagshaw is really smitten," Tacy announced.

"Well," Betsy answered jubilantly, "she says he isn't a *Lausbube*!"

The news grew even better. "Mr. Bagshaw had to go to New York but he hurried back here like mad."

"Tib likes him. She says he appreciates . . . listen to this . . . ! he *appreciates* her giving him so much of her time."

"Flowers, dances, a Rolls Royce, and *he* appreciates!"

"Isn't that just like Tib?"

And later: "This almost settles it! She thinks he looks like John Drew!"

He really did, Betsy thought, resemble that aging matinee idol. He had the same thinning hair, perfect tie and spats, an urbane yet weary air. She reflected on this again later in the evening.

Usually they listened to the concert from a blanket spread on the grass. The real seats were in the pavilion, but there were listeners in carriages and automobiles all around and in canoes on the lake. Tonight the Kerrs left early and Joe and Betsy rented a canoe.

Floating under the stars with her head on Joe's shoulder, the music coming dreamily over the dark water, Betsy was thinking how wonderful it was to be married, when she gave a dismayed start. Could Tib float in this haze of joy with anyone so old and worldly as Mr. John Drew Bagshaw?

"Why, he doesn't even like canoes!"

He liked sailboats, though. Sam kept a sailboat on Lake Calhoun and all of them, including the New Yorker, found it very pleasant about sunset to be out on the gilded, bouncing water. The Crowd scrambled over the boat, dove again and again, and swam around and around, calling insults and challenges. Mr. Bagshaw did not swim. He polished his glasses and smilingly watched Tib.

In a shepherd's-check bathing suit, like no other on the lake, Tib was worth watching. She wore silk stockings instead of the usual cotton ones. Her pretty legs gleamed as she balanced gaily before her birdlike dive. (When modestly under water she peeled off the stockings, hanging them neatly on the boat, but she always put them on again, under water, before climbing back.)

Although Mr. Bagshaw never swam, he was an excellent sailor and looked trimly nautical in immaculate blue coat and white duck trousers. When he took the tiller, Sam's boat showed its heels to every other boat of its class. He held his own with the younger men at tennis, too.

"His forehand is classic," Joe said. "His backhand is murder. If only he weren't always so anxious to win!" For Joe and Sam, although they battled furiously, never really cared who won.

"Probably he wants to impress Tib," said Betsy.

"No! It's the same ruthless drive that made him a millionaire."

"You like him, don't you?" she urged, a little anxiously.

"Sure! Sure!" Joe said.

They all did, in spite of his handicap of wealth and position. He tried so hard to be one of the Crowd that they were almost sorry for him. He did not know how to join in their crazy banter. At first he did not even understand the wild rush for a popcorn wagon.

These inviting vehicles paraded the summer streets, whistling shrilly, trailing savory smells. After he understood, Mr. Bagshaw made a point of stopping every one. With a great affectation of boyishness he brought dozens of buttery bags back to the Rolls Royce.

He liked to be out in his big automobile, perhaps because Tib was so delighted to be driving it. Yellow hair bare, she settled herself behind the wheel with an amusing air of efficiency. Mr. Bagshaw sat sidewise, smiling at her.

The Crowd took him to see all the sights.

Fort Snelling, high on a bluff above the meeting of the Mississippi and Minnesota Rivers! The old fort had seen almost a hundred years of history, the Crowd announced.

Minnehaha Falls! They were as well known in Europe as Teddy Roosevelt, Betsy said. Because of Longfellow, of course. She started to name the many people to whom she had promised postcard pictures of the Falls but she did not finish. Too many of them were in trenches or war-blackened cities.

Lake Minnetonka! One Sunday afternoon they

called on the Kerrs. Joe and Betsy reached for each other's hands at the first sight of the little green cottage on stilts.

Harry and Tacy hospitably brought coffee and cake out to the lawn but, as soon as she could, Tacy took Betsy aside. Her news was sobering.

"Mr. Bagshaw's business here is finished, Harry says. He could go back to New York if he wanted to. He just doesn't want to . . . without Tib."

"Without Tib?"

"Without Tib!"

New York seemed suddenly very far away.

"He'll propose before he goes back, as sure as shooting," Tacy said.

"Hmm!" said Betsy. Pushing her hands deep into the pockets of a green cardigan sweater, she looked across at the Japanese boathouse.

"Hmm!" said Tacy.

That very evening Mr. Bagshaw invited them all to a farewell dinner dance at the Inn on Christmas Lake. This sophisticated inn, which pretended to be rustic because it was in the country, was one of his favorite places.

It was to be a gala party, merrily jangling telephones reported over the next few days. Orchids for the ladies, and souvenirs . . . would they prefer gold mesh bags or vanity boxes? Tib asked seriously.

Joe insisted that Betsy must have a new dress. He had proposed that before, but Betsy always said she had plenty of dresses. As a matter of fact, the clothes fund had leaked mysteriously into the grocery fund . . . or off to the dentist.

"The budget just won't allow a new dress," she admitted at last.

Joe swung his shoulders. "The budget," he said, "isn't buying you this dress."

"Then how . . ."

"My bonuses," he answered.

The *Courier* gave a bonus for the best news story every week. A five dollar bonus, and Joe had been winning and had kept all his prize money out of both budget and savings account.

"For a new dress," he explained now. So he and Betsy went downtown and picked out a white chiffon with a blue velvet bodice. The flounces were edged with blue velvet, and blue velvet ribbons tied a malines ruff around her neck.

"I never felt so married as I did when I paid the clerk for that dress," Joe remarked as he watched Betsy prinking on the night of the dance. He also was pleased with everything that made him feel married.

"Do I look nice?"

"Like a dream!"

He was putting on the white coat he wore with blue trousers to summer parties when the doorbell rang and Betsy went to answer it. On the threshold stood a tall, handsome, smartly dressed girl with a mischievous expression. Peering over her shoulder were lively green eyes.

"Cab!" Betsy shouted joyfully. "And this is Jean!"

"My Missus!" he answered proudly, and Joe ran out and they all pumped one another's hands. Cab had been an important member of the old Deep Valley Crowd. His solid dependability was engagingly wrapped in rollicking high spirits.

He looked just the same, Betsy thought as they went inside—slim, springy, and neat as a bandbox. But when he took off his shining straw hat . . . ! Where was his thick black hair?

Cab followed her gaze. "I admit it," he said. "But I'm not as bald as I was the first time Jean saw me."

Jean laughed, a throaty contagious laugh. "Tell them about it, Cab," she said. Everyone sat down.

"Well, I was losing my hair. And someone told me that the way to make your hair grow was to shave your head. I was making a business trip way out to North Dakota, and it seemed a good time to try this cure, so I had my head shaved."

"There wasn't a spear left!" cried Jean. "Not a spear!"

"The first night there, I was out with the fellow I'd come to see, a nice chap from Georgia. Reb and I ran into Jean and another girl. Reb knew them and introduced me. Of course I started to take off my hat, but then I noticed what a wow Jean was, and I kept it on."

"I wondered why," said Jean, her throaty chuckle tumbling out again.

"Reb had an auto, and we all went for a ride. That was fine. I could keep my hat on. But when we stopped at an ice cream parlor I simply had to take it off."

"And I thought . . ." Jean's voice sank to a calamitous whisper. "I thought, 'The guy's bald-headed!'"

She and Cab both burst into laughter.

"He was cute," Jean insisted. "Bald head and all. And when he went back to Minnesota he sent me one of those boxes of chocolates a yard long."

"I had to work fast," Cab explained. "She was going off to Boston to study elocution."

"He liked my family," Jean said, winking.

"You bet I did!" Cab grew solemn. "Especially her mother. And my mother used to say to me, 'Caleb, when you go to pick out a wife, look at her mother!'"

"And did you?" Betsy asked breathlessly.

Cab rubbed his head. "Well, I didn't have much time to look at her very hard. I was too busy looking at Jean."

And they went off into laughter again.

She's just the one for him! Betsy thought.

"Say, Betsy," Cab said, "wasn't it swell that we got married the same day? Let's celebrate our anniversary together some time. You two come down to our little house in Deep Valley. Jean likes Deep Valley, and of course I love it, but I wish there were more of the old Crowd around."

At the word Crowd, Betsy dashed to the telephone. And when Tib learned who was sitting in the Willard living room, she said just what Betsy had hoped she would say.

"Oh, bring them to the dance! Please do! Rick would want them."

So Betsy went back to report a Crowd party that night.

"It's your chance, Cab, to introduce Jean to every-one."

"Who's giving it?" Cab asked.

"Oh, a New York millionaire who's in love with Tib."

Jean hooked her arm in Cab's. "I hope," she said, "he's as nice as my struggling young business man."

"Not struggling to get away from you, angel!"

For some reason this light-hearted exchange made Betsy feel blue.

She felt blue driving out to Christmas Lake, although the Hutchinsons had picked them up and there was more joyful excitement over Cab and Jean. These welcome visitors enlivened the party, too, but Betsy felt bluer and bluer through the whole superlative affair.

As usual, in a smart restaurant Mr. Bagshaw was at his gleaming best. As usual, he had secured a table next to the dance floor, the waiters were hypnotized by his re-gal air, and the orchestra leader hurried over to pay his respects. There were boutonnieres for the men, as well as orchids for the ladies. There was a mesh bag even for the unexpected Jean.

Betsy was glad of the new chiffon, for everyone wore something special. Tacy's black and white striped taffeta, with white blouse and black bolero jacket, brought out her autumn coloring. Carney's cool marquisette had the simplicity she loved. Tib had thrown together a yellow silk marvel. Below a tight vestee, dozens of tiny ruffles raced down to her ankles.

"I painted the slippers to match," she confided, extending a tiny foot.

Although Mr. Bagshaw was usually so polite, he did not dance with anyone but Tib. When she danced with someone else, he watched. He pulled out the leather cigarette case, passed it absently, and selected a cigarette, hardly removing his eyes from those whirling yellow ruffles.

"He'll propose tonight. I feel it in my bones," Tacy whispered glumly.

And sure enough, when the orchestra rested and the Crowd moved out to the broad piazza, he asked Tib to walk down to the lake. He very pointedly did not suggest that anyone else come along, although the lake shimmered under a full August moon. He and Tib strolled off through a warm darkness filled with the flashings of fireflies. They disappeared down rustic stairs leading to the water.

Betsy and Tacy sat close together for comfort. Tacy burst out: "I had the fun of marrying for love!"

"So did I!" said Betsy. "I should say I did!"

"So did Jean."

Jean joined them. She asked in a mirthful whisper, "Who is he? He freezes my bones."

The orchestra began to play "Araby" and the Crowd went back to the dance floor . . . except for the two who had gone down to the lake.

The orchestra played "You're Here, and I'm Here, so What Do We Care?" But Tib wasn't there, and Betsy and Tacy found that they cared terribly. Why had it seemed such a fine idea for Tib to marry a New York millionaire?

The orchestra played "Pack Up Your Troubles," and for the first time that summer Betsy and Tacy felt they really had a trouble to pack. Tib and Mr. Bagshaw returned. His face was inscrutable, as always. Tib had been crying. She had powdered; she was smiling; but she had been crying. Betsy and Tacy looked at each other with stricken eyes.

Why had she been crying? Because she had turned him down? Tib was very tender-hearted. Or because she was going to New York to live in lonely grandeur?

The evening ended without any chance for intimate conversation. The dressing room was crowded with chattering women.

Mr. Bagshaw bent over their hands with his customary urbanity. Tib's farewells were a little subdued, and they drove off in the big impressive car.

The Kerrs followed. Sam and Carney delivered Cab and Jean to their hotel, then dropped the Willards off at their apartment. And when Joe and Betsy went in, they found a special delivery letter in their mailbox.

12

A LETTER FROM AUNT RUTH

The letter was from Aunt Ruth. Joe tore it open as they went upstairs, and inside the apartment Betsy dropped into a rocker and waited. Her cheeks, above the chiffon dress, were still flushed from the party.

Joe sat down in his blue chair and read aloud. The letter was short but its impact was powerful. Aunt Ruth had sold Willard's Emporium to Homer. He had been married, and he and his wife were going to live in the rooms above the store. He had bought the furniture.

"I feel all upset," Aunt Ruth wrote. "Selling out was hard on me, and I don't know what to do next. I wish I could come and stay with you folks."

That was all, except "Your loving Aunt."

Joe put the letter down and looked at Betsy, his eyes troubled.

"We'll have to let her come," he said.

"Why—why—how can we?" Betsy faltered. He couldn't know what he was saying. Let her come? Let anyone invade their Paradise? "We—haven't room for her," she added lamely, choosing the least important of the many objections hammering at her heart.

"We'll have to find room," Joe said. "That isn't what bothers me. It's asking so much of you, Betsy, that makes me feel bad. But I can't say no. It isn't as though she wanted to live with us indefinitely. She probably just wants a chance to make some plans. And I'm the only relative she has—around here, I mean."

"You're not exactly a relative," Betsy said in a choked voice. "You were Uncle Alvin's nephew."

"She didn't think about that when they let me come to live with them."

But Joe, Betsy thought rebelliously, had paid his own way. He had worked in the store, and after he was ready for high school, he had moved to Deep Valley and supported himself.

Joe read her thoughts. "I know I always helped around

the place. But just the way their own son would have done. In Deep Valley I worked, of course, but I spent Sundays and holidays out at Butternut Center. And Aunt Ruth never let me go back without a basket full of apples, or cookies, or a fruit cake. I sent my mending to her—laundry, too, sometimes. And often when she wrote to me she'd stick in a dollar bill. Now she's feeling lost and wants to be with family for a while. I can't refuse her, Betsy."

Betsy gazed around the little honeymoon apartment. It looked sweeter than it had ever looked before. The glow of lamplight rested on the old chairs, the books, her grandfather's table. The elm tree beyond the bay window was swallowed up in the night, but she could feel it out there.

"Our lease is up next month. That's a good thing. We can rent a place with more room. Betsy!" Joe looked up, and his voice took on a new note. "We've saved some money. Maybe we could make a down payment on a house? Pay for it like rent?"

Betsy heard the lift in his voice. She wanted to reply with warmth, with enthusiasm, but she couldn't seem to do it. She couldn't bring herself to speak at all.

Joe pushed both hands over a worried forehead. "Oh, we can't afford it, I guess! I wish I'd get another raise," he said in a discouraged tone.

Betsy couldn't stand that. She got up and crossed the room and kissed him. But she kissed him quickly and went to hang up her coat.

"You're earning plenty," she said. "And I think we have enough for a down payment. We have over five hundred dollars. If we have to pay more by the month than we're paying Mrs. Hilton, we can add what we're putting in the savings now. I can juggle the budget."

But Joe knew that her brisk cheerfulness was false. He followed her out to the foyer and put his arms around her.

"Thank you, Betsy," he said. He sounded humble.

They did not talk any more but got ready for bed quickly. Usually, after a party, Betsy hated to undress. It was as sad as dismantling a Christmas tree, she would say, admiring herself in the mirror from all angles, and when she had taken off her dress, she would pull the pins out of her hair slowly, and shake it around her shoulders and pose until Joe came, laughing, to stop her.

Tonight she took off the new dress promptly and was soon in bed.

She lay in Joe's arms a few minutes and then he went to sleep, but Betsy could not sleep. She felt overwhelmed. It wasn't that she minded buying a house, living more cheaply, giving up luxuries . . . none of that mattered at all. Besides, she was confident Joe's salary would rise to any need. What she minded was giving up their delicious privacy, the fun of it being just the two of them, keeping house all alone. She wouldn't mind giving it up for a baby, but for anything else she would.

"Why couldn't it have been a baby?" she asked, and a few tears dripped into her pillow.

But she remembered the eagerness in Joe's voice when he had mentioned buying a house, and how she had quenched it. She remembered his humble, "Thank you, Betsy." He had thanked her just for accepting his decision; he knew as well as she did that she had done it grudgingly.

It was the best I could manage, Betsy thought, still crying a little. But next morning at breakfast she tried harder.

"I'll tell Mrs. Hilton today that we won't be renewing," she said, brightly casual. "Will you write Aunt Ruth, or shall I?"

"I'll write from the office," Joe replied. "And maybe you'll have time to call some real estate men?"

"As soon as I get the family officially welcomed." The Rays were arriving from California. "I'm taking them a cake."

"It will be fine to see them."

Joe was brightly casual, too. But he was unhappy. Betsy could see it in his eyes and in the way—after he had kissed her good-by—he squared his shoulders, and ran downstairs, and went swinging out into the street.

She washed and wiped the dishes and hung the tea towels to dry. She made the cake and it turned out well, and she ran the carpet sweeper up and down, pausing, as usual, to look out into the elm. She looked for a long time.

I love that tree, Betsy thought. Last night's tears

came back and ran slowly down her cheeks. She went to the bathroom and washed them off, and powdered.

The telephone rang, and it was Joe.

"You all right, Betsy?"

"Why, of course! Almost ready to start for the train."

"I just thought I'd like to talk with you," he said. There was a pause. "I've written to Aunt Ruth."

"That's good. And don't worry, dear." She tried to put the proper reassurance into her voice but she knew she hadn't succeeded.

"I love you, Betsy," Joe said softly.

"I love you, too."

After she put down the receiver, she cried some more.

Tacy telephoned, wanting to know whether Betsy had heard from Tib. Betsy didn't tell the news about Aunt Ruth. Tacy would have been a good one to tell. She was unfailingly tactful. But she would be sorry, and Betsy didn't want to be pitied.

She didn't tell her family, although it was comforting to see them. Mr. Ray's smiling face was tanned by the California sun.

"And look at my freckles!" Mrs. Ray cried. Her red hair curled beneath a broad-brimmed hat. "I bought this hat, and wore gloves, and carried an umbrella all summer. But look at me!"

"And look at me!" laughed Margaret. Margaret did, indeed, have a new sprinkle on her nose. And that wasn't the only way she had changed. She had a new shy sparkle.

"Boy cousins!" Mrs. Ray whispered, walking toward the taxi. "Two of them, just her age. They teased her and flirted with her and tore her dignity to tatters."

Louisa was waiting on the Ray front steps.

"Bogie!" she shouted and catapulted into Margaret's hug. They rushed to find Anna, who had returned the day before—and Kismet. The goldfish were back above the bookcase and Kismet stood with a paw on either side of the bowl looking contentedly downward.

Margaret and Louisa disappeared, but Betsy and her parents sat on the back porch and drank coffee and ate Betsy's cake. She had felt a little foolish, bringing it, because of Anna, but it seemed the sort of gesture a married daughter should make. They talked and talked and Betsy almost forgot Aunt Ruth in the news of her grandmother, and the two Expositions.

When she said that she had to go home and start dinner, Mrs. Ray telephoned Joe.

"Anna has peaches for a shortcake."

"Lady, I'll be there!"

He came in, smiling broadly, although he gave Betsy an anxious look when he kissed her. And after the short-cake, presents were brought out. The Willards were given a pottery hanging basket.

"For flowers and vines," Mrs. Ray explained. "I thought it would be pretty in your bay window."

"It would be lovely anywhere," Betsy said.

Joe reached for her hand. "I guess Betsy hasn't told you. We're thinking of buying a house."

"You're giving up that darling apartment?" Mrs. Ray exclaimed.

"We need more room. No . . ." He grinned. "It's not a baby! My Aunt Ruth wants to come and stay with us a while."

"She's sold the store and feels lonesome," Betsy explained, striving for a natural tone.

She knew, without looking at her parents, what their reactions to the news would be. Mrs. Ray would think it was too bad, although she would not say so, and she would agree that Betsy should do whatever her husband thought best. Mr. Ray would approve. Sure enough, he spoke heartily.

"That's a mighty kind thing for you kids to do."

Walking home, Joe said, "Your father took me out on the porch, while you were telling your mother about Bagshaw's party. He wanted to loan us money enough for our down payment. It was grand of him, but I'd rather not borrow. How about you?"

"I wouldn't like to either," Betsy said. "Saving out a couple of hundred dollars for the extra furniture we'll need, we could still pay down three hundred dollars."

But when they started house hunting, they found that three hundred dollars was considered very meager.

They met discouragement everywhere, but at least Tib's news was good.

"Why, of course, I turned him down!" she said. It was on the telephone. "Did you think for a moment that I wouldn't? He's very nice, and I liked him, and I adored his car, but *marry* him! *Lieber Gott!*"

"Better luck next time," Betsy joked to Tacy, passing on the news of their failure. They were immeasurably relieved.

Joe was amused, and he and Betsy discussed Mr. Bagshaw's exit at some length. Any fresh topic seemed welcome these days. There was a strange new feeling in the Willard apartment.

Betsy couldn't quite understand it. They were loving to each other, as always. Both of them made an unusual effort to be entertaining. Perhaps that was what made the strangeness? Or perhaps it was just because they weren't happy? But the feeling grew like a thickening fog.

Betsy went house hunting every day, alone and with real estate agents. But she had no success. On any house that pleased her, the owner wanted more than three hundred dollars down.

"Maybe we'll have to rent after all," Joe said.

He never suggested holding Aunt Ruth off, and Betsy did not even hint at such a solution, but in her reveries the prospect of Aunt Ruth grew darker and darker.

She would have to be included in all their parties, and she wouldn't fit in at all. She wouldn't have any interest in their friends, or they in her. She would sit around and listen to Joe and Betsy talk. What about their little private jokes, the tender intimacies they were in the habit of exchanging as they cooked or washed dishes or sat together in the evenings? Even the reading aloud would not have the same flavor, with Aunt Ruth listening, too.

The grimmer her thoughts were, the harder Betsy tried to find a house. Getting tired over that search eased her conscience a little. And her conscience hurt sharply. It was almost terrible that it should be so hard to reconcile herself to Joe's wishes.

I wouldn't have believed it! she thought.

She said her prayers fiercely, and Saturday night she decided that church would help, so next morning she slipped out of bed early. Joe roused up but she whispered, "Go back to sleep. I'm going to church."

He murmured, "Say a prayer for me, honey."

"I will. I always do."

It had turned cold in the night. Flowers were frozen, there was hoarfrost on the lawns. Betsy had always loved this early service, partly because it took her out into such a fresh and empty world. But this morning she only wanted to get to church.

She wanted to wrench out, if she could, her hateful resentment about Aunt Ruth.

I agreed to let her come, yes. But "the gift without the giver is bare," she told herself angrily, hurrying along.

She could hear her father's voice. "That's mighty kind of you kids." But she didn't feel kind. She wished she did; but she didn't.

Inside St. Paul's, she flung herself down on her knees. The church was almost empty. Morning light came through green-and-yellow windows and made a pattern on the clean white walls. It was a plain church—plain brown choir stalls, a plain cross on the altar. The service began.

"Almighty God, unto whom all hearts are open. . . ."

Betsy dug her head into her arms. "Help me, God! Please help me!" she prayed.

This was the first real problem of their marriage. Up to now, everything had been perfect. Her struggles with cooking, Joe's low moods hadn't mattered, really. This was different. It was a real disagreement.

Joe had decided it. "But I wanted him to. One person in a family has to have the final word. I want it to be Joe, always."

If only he could have decided that they didn't have room for Aunt Ruth . . . that it was too bad, but she would have to manage some other way. . . .

That thought brought Betsy's head up, sharply.

Would she really have liked that, she asked herself? Why—why—it wouldn't have been Joe! How would she like Joe not being Joe? If she needed him, or someone in her own family needed him, how would she like Joe not being Joe? What would it be like, not to be sure, always, that Joe would do whatever he thought was right?

All of a sudden everything came clear.

The beautiful ritual unfolded, and Betsy began to make the responses, a little absently, but with a heart so full of love and thankfulness, she knew God wouldn't mind. She felt all right. She felt like herself. When the service ended, she went home on flying feet.

Joe, in his dressing gown, was sitting in the blue easy chair, with the Real Estate section of the paper. His face looked worried, but it changed when he saw Betsy's face. He stood up, and she came over and slipped her arms underneath his so she could hug him tightly. She put her head down on his chest.

"Joe," she said, "I feel all right about Aunt Ruth. I mean—I think it's the right thing to do. I don't mind, anymore."

"Oh, Betsy!" Joe said. He sounded as though he'd like to cry. They hugged each other until Betsy broke away.

"See here!" she said. "I don't smell coffee. What kind of a husband are you, anyway?" She shook him. "I'll make some. And you get dressed. And we'll go find us a house."

"If there's anything I don't like, it's a bossy woman," Joe said, and pulled her back into his arms.

After breakfast Betsy put on her green cardigan over the ruffled blouse and green plaid skirt Joe liked. Swinging hands, they started out.

Previously they had decided that the Bow Street neighborhood was too expensive for them. They had been searching farther out. All Joe's clippings from the paper today were for more distant places. But now, instead of taking the streetcar, they headed for the lakes.

"We're at home in this part of town. Let's give it a try," Joe said.

The hoarfrost was gone. Sunshine gleamed on lawns and sidewalks. They crossed Hennepin Avenue at a small business district and were walking toward Lake of the Isles when Betsy stopped. She waved toward a short street that cut off a pie-shaped section of more important avenues.

"I think that Canoe Place is cute," she said, "because it's only a block long."

Then she squealed, and Joe said, "Well, for crying out loud!" For on a lawn halfway down Canoe Place was a For Sale sign. They started to run.

The brown-and-yellow cottage was set on a very small lot. It didn't have a barn or a garage. At the back rose the back of a tall apartment building, but there were only houses on Canoe Place itself. There were maple trees along it, and the cottage had a neat lawn, cut in two by a walk leading to the porch.

The porch was big; it was screened. "We could eat out there," Betsy said, "all summer long."

The porch door was locked and the house was plainly empty. They walked around to the left side and saw lofty leaded windows.

"They'll be over a built-in buffet. That must be the

dining room. The kitchen's behind, probably," Betsy decided.

On the right side were two large windows and one small leaded one. They peeked in on what was certainly a living room. The leaded window rose above a turn of the stairs.

They squinted at the upstairs windows.

"Must be three bedrooms," Joe said.

They walked around in back and Betsy clutched Joe's arm. "Darling! An apple tree!"

The apples were red, and there was a birdhouse in the branches.

The For Sale sign directed Joe and Betsy to a Mr. Munson on nearby Hennepin Avenue. They rushed off to find him.

Mr. Munson reminded them both of Mr. Ray.

"Yes, young folks, that's a good little house."

"What does it sell for?" Joe asked.

"Four thousand, five hundred."

"We could stand good monthly payments," Joe said. "And we're responsible people. I'm on the *Courier*. But we can't pay much down."

"Just three hundred dollars," Betsy put in.

Mr. Munson tapped his teeth thoughtfully with a pencil. "I don't believe," he said, "that the size of the down payment matters much in this case. The owners are old people; well fixed; going to California. I think it could be arranged."

Joe looked at Betsy, blue eyes snapping. Her hazel eyes were snapping too, and color was dancing in her cheeks.

"Did you bring the checkbook, honey?"

"Yes, dear." She drew it out of her bag.

"Whoa!" said Mr. Munson. "I can't show you that house today. I can't get a key until tomorrow."

"We looked in the windows," Betsy explained politely.

"They might as well have our three hundred dollars, sir," said Joe, taking out his pen.

"I won't cash that check," said Mr. Munson, "until you can look through the house. Of course, it's all right. It really is. A good hot water furnace. Hardwood floors."

He stopped for they weren't listening.

Joe was proudly waving the check to dry it, and Betsy looked off with dreamy eyes. She was thinking about the apple tree, and the apples. And the birdhouse, too, of course.

13

NIGHT LIFE FOR THE WILLARDS

"Next spring," said Mr. Ray, "I'll make a cutting of that vine I brought from Deep Valley. I'll plant it beside your front porch."

He surveyed the new Willard home with a smiling satisfaction which was shared by all the Rays.

The Crowd inspected 7 Canoe Place with eager interest; Joe and Betsy were the first ones to buy a house. Everyone went upstairs and down through the shiny, empty rooms and even into the basement—all but Tib, who lingered in the kitchen.

"You could really cook here, Betsy," she said. "I'll come sometime and roast you a duck with apple dressing."

Anna, too, when she came to help Betsy paper the shelves, smiled on the big, sunny room. "This is a good kitchen to have a cup of coffee in, lovey," she said. And coffee they had often through September, sitting happily on packing boxes, for Joe and Betsy moved by degrees from the apartment to the new house.

They came over every day with linen for the linen closet, or clothes for the clothes closets, or just to walk proudly around their new domain.

"This," Betsy said, standing in the smallest bedroom, "will be the study—until we need it for a nursery, that is. We'll hang the Harvard etchings here."

"And the long-legged bird," said Joe.

"No, I'm going to write in our bedroom, beside the window that looks down on our apple tree."

He nodded, munching one of the apples. "Wonderful flavor!" he remarked in an aside.

It was delightful, planning the rooms, but troubling, too. For the apartment furniture would make only a spatter in this mansion. And there were so many, many windows! White, ruffled curtains all over the house would be both charming and inexpensive, but rugs were a more serious matter. Betsy and her mother scoured the secondhand stores, ending triumphantly with two ancient orientals. In living room and dining room, their faded colors glowed.

The blue rug from the apartment would go into their bedroom, Joe and Betsy planned. And their white bedroom furniture would look very well there. But what would they put in the third bedroom, equally large, assigned to Aunt Ruth? Their savings were sinking like water in a sand hole. They had bought a dining room set on monthly payments.

"And there mustn't be any more of *that*!" Betsy said.

The problem was still unsolved when their wedding anniversary came around.

Joe brought home a box of red roses and Betsy put one radiantly into her hair, but after dinner they went over to Canoe Place to settle their books in the built-in bookcases. They were busy with this blissful task when they heard a motor car. It was the Hawthornes.

"We just stopped by to tell you we remembered," Mrs. Hawthorne said, in a mirthfully affectionate tone. "It's paper, isn't it, for the first anniversary?" She extended Donn Byrne's *Messer Marco Polo*.

"Oh, thank you!" cried Betsy. "I haven't read it."

"I have. And I'm certainly glad to own it."

"Well, where shall we put it?" Brad Hawthorne dropped down beside the pile of books. He and Joe began to browse, and Betsy showed Mrs. Hawthorne over the house. In Aunt Ruth's room she explained:

"We're still shopping for this one. We do want it to

please her, but we can't spend much. Joe and I just won't go into debt."

Mrs. Hawthorne looked around. "Does Aunt Ruth like old-fashioned things?"

"Oh, yes! She's very old-fashioned."

"Then we have just the set! It's been gathering dust in our attic for years. Come on! We'll go look at it."

And, running downstairs, she and Betsy pulled the men into the motor car. At the tall peaked house among the oaks, they ran up two flights of stairs, joined by Sally Day in yellow pajamas.

The lofty headboard of the old black walnut bed was covered with ornate carving, and so were the bureau, the chest, and the washstand, which had a marble top.

"Of course, we'll pay you for it," Joe said.

"Nonsense!" Mrs. Hawthorne answered. "We've no use for it. I've just had a sentiment about giving it away. But you two seem like our own children."

"Do me a favor! Take it!" her husband hissed.

"If you take it," Sally Day chimed, "I'll have more room for the circus I'm giving up here. I'm going to do tricks. Want to see some?"

"It's all decided, and now we'll celebrate with waffles." Mrs. Hawthorne led the way to the kitchen.

She stirred up batter—Joe advised the addition of a sprinkle of nutmeg. He made coffee while Mr. Hawthorne read aloud from *Penrod,* and Betsy set the dining room table with green glass dishes trimmed in silver. Sally Day was sent to bed and came bouncing back, was sent to bed again and again came bouncing back, and at last was allowed one waffle—butter and syrup unlimited!

On the day the movers brought the furniture from the Willard apartment they went to the Hawthornes' and picked up the old bedroom set.

It was thrilling to see the furniture put into place in the new house. Numerous bare spots remained, but Joe and Betsy filled them mentally with things which would come later—a piano here, a phonograph there, a couch . . ! The porch was still empty but it would be ridiculous, Betsy said, to furnish an open porch in the fall. Next spring they would buy a swing, and wicker chairs and tables.

Joe, who had taken the day off, rushed about with a tack hammer. Betsy rushed about with Goethe's cup, Joe's mother's vase, the angel from Oberammergau, and other treasures she was afraid to put down.

Coal was delivered. It rattled into the basement bin and Joe ran down to watch while Betsy listened, smiling, to the cozy sound!

She was sweeping colored maple leaves off their front walk, when Joe came out briskly.

"I started a fire. We don't really need it. But I thought I'd better get acquainted with that furnace."

"It's a fine idea," Betsy said.

Eating baked beans and pumpkin pie that Anna had

sent for their supper, they listened proudly to the sizzle of heat in their radiators. And before going to bed they went out on the porch and looked up at a misty moon.

"Joe!" said Betsy. "Isn't it wonderful to have our own house?"

"Now that we've taken the plunge," he confided, "I'm scared."

"Now that we've taken the plunge, we'll swim."

"It may be hard swimming. Gol darn newspaper salaries!"

"You wouldn't be anything but a newspaper man. And I wouldn't have you be, until you can be an author."

"I could use a raise," Joe said dourly.

The next night when he came home for the first time to 7 Canoe Place, to candles on the dining room table and Betsy in a hastily-tied-on frothy apron, he was grinning, but the grin was dour.

"Well, the Lord and Brad Hawthorne helped us out! I have a raise."

"Joe Willard!" Betsy hugged and shook him. "What's the matter? Why aren't you pleased?"

"I am pleased. But it's night work. Six to two."

"Why, we won't mind that! I'll keep the same hours you do. It will be sort of interesting, working and living at night. Sit down and tell me about it."

Joe sat down, frowning. "What I don't like, really, is that I won't be writing."

"You won't be writing!"

"I'll be on the copy desk. I worked there while I was going to the U, you remember. I'm good at editing copy, writing heads."

"But you're good at writing stories, too. You're wonderful! It isn't worth the extra money," Betsy cried indignantly.

"We can use ten dollars more a week. It will settle all our worries." He reached out for her hand. "Don't think I'm blue. This raise makes me think somehow that we're doing the right thing."

Betsy didn't answer. It was strange, she thought, how things worked out. Something was given to you but something was taken away. An apple tree for an elm tree. A raise, but you lost the chance to do what you really wanted to do. Joe was a *writer*.

He was stroking her hand. "Maybe," he said, "this new setup will give me more time for fiction."

Betsy looked up. Her hazel eyes, which had been close to tears, grew luminous.

"Of course!" she said. "Of course! I was just trying to think it through. Good things come, but they're never perfect; are they? You have to twist them into something perfect."

Joe laughed. "You have to wrestle with them," he said. "Like Jacob with the angel." Joe hadn't gone to church very much but he knew the Bible better than Betsy did.

"What about Jacob and the angel?"

"Why, Jacob took a grip on him and said, 'I will not let thee go, except thou bless me.'"

"Well, we won't let this job go until it blesses you!" Betsy cried. "And I don't mean any old ten dollars a week. You can sleep until noon and then go into that little study and shut the door and pound your typewriter . . ." She stopped, sniffed, and shrieked.

"My pork chops! Burning on!"

She dashed for the kitchen and Joe followed, chortling. "Well, at least it isn't a meat pie!"

He was to begin his new work Sunday, and that afternoon Aunt Ruth arrived. She was welcomed according to Ray tradition—Willard tradition now—with a shining house, a gala dinner.

Following Tacy's example, Betsy had long since learned a company dinner. Scalloped potatoes cooked with ham, canned peas, a moulded salad, muffins, and a lemon meringue pie. Everything but the muffins could be prepared ahead of time. She baked them after the return from the depot while Aunt Ruth rested.

Aunt Ruth seemed tired when Joe put her bulging bags down in her bedroom. She pushed back wisps of hair and looked around, almost bewildered, at the big soft bed under a snowy comforter, the old bureau with its bouquet of petunias, the washstand turned into a bedside table for magazines and a shaded lamp.

But she came down to dinner wearing a black silk dress with a handmade lace collar, her grayish hair smoothly brushed. She looked nice.

"The minute I touched that bed, I went to sleep," she

said. She was carrying presents for Joe and Betsy; a jar of watermelon pickles, pillow cases with crocheted lace edges, a big silver coffee pot.

"Alvin gave me that for our silver wedding, and I want you children to have it," she said, smiling at their pleasure.

She didn't eat much, but her eyes were bright as she looked around the pretty table.

Joe left for work—it was twilight and other husbands were coming home. Aunt Ruth went to bed early. The house seemed strange that night. But Betsy knew that she and Joe would adjust more easily to a third member in the household because their routine had changed so drastically.

As soon as Aunt Ruth seemed at home, Betsy began to keep Joe's hours. They all shared an early dinner, and after the dishes were washed, Aunt Ruth crocheted. Betsy brought out her mending basket, but Aunt Ruth took possession of it.

"I'm used to mending," she said.

Crocheting or mending, she wore a shawl, for no matter how warm the house was kept, Aunt Ruth was always cold. And through the long evenings, she talked and Betsy listened.

Betsy had loved her grandmother's stories and she loved Aunt Ruth's now. Stories about Joe's father, about his beautiful mother, even about Joe when he was a baby. Stories about Uncle Alvin's wooing, about the death—

stillborn—of their only child, about the elopement of Aunt Ruth's sister.

There's a plot in every one, Betsy thought, and started taking notes.

Fires, blizzards, grasshopper plagues went into that notebook. Aunt Ruth loved disasters. But she was far from gloomy even though her usual expression was sad. She laughed and laughed when she told of barn raisings and bobsled parties. She laughed until she cried over Betsy's meat pie.

Always, after the stories, they made tea. Astonishingly Aunt Ruth preferred tea to coffee. They took this snack in the kitchen where sometimes bread was baking.

Copying country-bred Mr. Ray, who always "put down" staple foods for the winter, Joe and Betsy had stored in their basement a barrel of apples, and baskets of potatoes, turnips, and onions. But it was Aunt Ruth's idea to lay in a big sack of flour.

"In Butternut Center they used to say, 'Uneeda loaf of Ruth Willard's bread,' " she told them roguishly.

Betsy watched with interest the kneading down and rising up of the dough. It was cut and shaped into loaves which were greased and put in the oven. While they baked, the kitchen filled with a mouth-watering smell. The golden brown loaves were put on a clean cloth and buttered.

"I remember Tacy's mother doing that," Betsy said. "When the bread cooled, she'd give me a piece."

So did Aunt Ruth, a thick one, with butter and honey.

After Aunt Ruth went to bed, Betsy changed to a house dress and put her hair in curlers. She got out the dust mop and carpet sweeper. And when all was neat, she sat down at her desk. The apple tree was lost in shadows, but she saw the lighted windows of the tall apartment building behind the cottage. She watched the windows darken, one by one. A single one, like her own, stayed bright all night. How friendly!

Betsy's forefingers pounced on the typewriter keys.

Before Joe came home she powdered and perfumed and did her hair. She made cocoa and sandwiches and set a table for two. Sometimes she put on a coat and went out to the porch to watch for him. The stars were sharp and bright above a sleeping world.

Joe would come in, stamping his feet, his face cold when he kissed her. As he ate he told her what good heads he had written, news of the Great War. And Betsy passed along Aunt Ruth's tales. Sometimes one of these had provided a plot for the story she was writing. Sometimes one of them flashed into a plot for Joe. They sat and talked while the darkness outside paled. Often the sky was on fire before they went to bed.

After a noon breakfast (luncheon for Aunt Ruth), Joe shoveled snow or he and Betsy put out bread for the birds. Then he did what Betsy had prophesied. He went into his study, shut the door, and wrote. Afterwards he had a few free hours but other men were working, so the Willards did not see much of the Crowd.

Carney and Sam were busy, for Judy had a baby brother. And Tacy was going to have a second child in the summer. She came to tell Betsy the news.

"It will be so nice for Kelly," she said.

Kelly could talk now. Not just his parents understood him; seventeen words were plain to anyone. He staggered around on plump legs.

"Luscious as he is," Betsy cried, snatching him, "the next one must be a girl!"

"I have that doll packed away, waiting," Tacy laughed.

Often Joe, Betsy, and Aunt Ruth strolled over to the Rays'. They read letters from Julia and Paige, dizzy with the brilliance of New York's musical season. They heard Margaret's news.

She and Louisa, juniors this year, were going out with two good-looking boys who were also inseparable friends. The four went out interchangeably. One time it would be Bill and Bogie, Bub and Boogie. Next time it would be Bill and Boogie, Bub and Bogie. Betsy found the situation most confusing.

"Don't any of them mind?" she asked her mother.

"Not that I can see."

"When I was their age, I got crushes."

"Margaret doesn't seem to have any preference. And neither does Louisa, and neither do the boys. It's beyond me," Mrs. Ray said.

Soon Joe and Betsy were hanging a holly wreath on their front door. They were tying the small Santa Claus to mistletoe on their chandelier, and trimming a Christmas tree in that corner of the living room where after Christmas—this was Joe's secret—a phonograph would stand. Aunt Ruth was baking Christmas cookies of every shape and kind.

At the Ray Christmas, Aunt Ruth listened, tender-eyed, to the reading of the Bible story. She joined in the carol singing and attacked her bulging stocking with excited eagerness.

"I'd been dreading Christmas, but I was happy all day long," she told Betsy when they said good night.

Henry Ford had sent a Peace Ship to get the boys out of the trenches by Christmas. But he hadn't succeeded. And no Allied offensive had been able to break the German line. U-boats were still sinking neutral shipping. Americans grew less neutral all the time. Then some German plotting in the United States was exposed, and there was a rising suspicion of all German-Americans.

This was on Tib's mind when she came out to the Willards' late one Sunday afternoon. She had been skating with her brother Fred.

"We had such fun!" she exclaimed, shaking out of her wraps and pinning up her loosened hair. Tib was as expert on the ice as she was on the dance floor. "Fred and I could be exhibition skaters! Maybe we will be!" she boasted gaily. But at supper, with a sobering face, she brought up the German-American talk.

"I don't mind. You know I'm always philosophical. *Nicht wahr*, Betsy? But it's hard on my brothers, especially Hobbie."

Hobbie, born during the Spanish-American War, had been named for its naval hero, Hobson, but he was seldom called by that dignified moniker, being short and dimpled and full of mischief. He went to high school in Deep Valley where the Mullers lived.

"Hobbie says he's going up to Canada and enlist."

"Oh, I hope he won't do that!" cried Betsy.

"Well, Mamma's doing plenty of worrying! And so am I."

Next day Betsy telephoned Tacy.

"I know," she said, "our idea about Mr. Bagshaw was crazy. But Tib has this German-American business on her mind. And she doesn't give a snap for any of her beaus. Maybe we ought to try again."

Tacy chuckled. "Well, Harry and I did our best! Now it's up to you and Joe."

Betsy agreed. But she and Joe had little time for scouting. He had only one free evening weekly, and oftenest they gave it to a newspaper group that met at the Jimmy Cliffs' . . . to talk writing, read aloud, argue, and drink coffee while Jimmy Junior dashed up and down on his kiddy car.

In Minneapolis there was a sedate and ladylike group called the Violet Study Club. One night when the Willards and their friends were gathered at the Cliffs, and the kiddy car collided with hot coffee and an even hotter argument about Sherwood Anderson's work, the girl columnist "Q" remarked, "We ought to call this the *Violent* Study Club."

The name stuck.

If I find a husband for Tib, Betsy thought, it will be at the Violent Study Club.

14
AT THE VIOLENT STUDY CLUB

"First member to get both hands up reads first!" boomed President Jimmy Cliff.

Up and down the firelit living room, books, note-books, and pencils clattered to the floor as members hastened to obey the unexpected order for two hands. One plump, dimpled pair rose with suspicious ease and the President nodded at the plump, dimpled owner.

"You win, Patty. No doubt because I warned you. However, this club is all for cheating, so you may read. And how nice that you have brought one of my favorite books!"

Tib's bewildered voice came through the hubbub of protest. "But I never saw a club run like this! Don't you have any rules of order?"

"Miss Muller," answered the President, "this club is very anti rules of order."

"That two-hands stuff, though, was really under-hand!" Joe's pun brought jeers and groans.

"Mr. Willard! Do you deny your President the gratification of a momentary whim? Or to be plainer, do you want your fair share of the Cliff coffee and doughnuts? Read, Patty!"

But before she could begin, Jimmy Junior roared out on his kiddy car, yelling, "Pop! Bang! Pop!" His tall, slender mother rushed to carry him off to bed. His large, stout father, wedged into an oversized armchair, shook with laughter.

The Violent Study Club, which met whenever the spirit moved its members, was in session.

Tib was laughing now. "Why, I love this club!" she cried. "It's wonderful! It reminds me of that Okto Delta we had in high school. Doesn't it you, Betsy?"

Tib, Betsy thought admiringly, fitted into any group. She was never ill at ease, and so good-natured—falling in with other people's ways, laughing at their jokes, looking out for chances to be useful! She jumped up now to put away the kiddy car, but hurried back to her sofa, not to miss a word of the hilarious proceedings.

A black velvet dress swathed her from neck to ankles. She meant it, probably, to make her look like a vamp—a word brought into the language by the moving picture actress, Theda Bara. Tib's flowerlike face, flushed with fun, was not at all like Bara's, but she looked pretty enough to fascinate anyone.

Who was there, tonight, to fascinate? From her chair beside the fire, Betsy appraised the room. MacTavish, the bony Scot, whom everyone looked up to because he sold verse to magazines of quality (although for very little money), did not seem Tib's type. The pleasant, serious reporter was a bachelor, long confirmed. The magazine editor was very good-looking, but he had come with "Q."

Betsy had been surprised, when she first met "Q," to find her young, with shining hair and very pretty legs—although she was always pulling down her skirts. Only vivid blue eyes gave a hint of her wit.

Sigrid, the vivacious, nut-brown girl reporter, waved a left hand on which a diamond shone.

"If Jimmy likes Patty's book, we all smell Dickens!" she cried above the uproar.

Patty and Jimmy both loved Dickens; and Dickens would have loved them, Betsy thought. Jimmy's face, above his flowing Windsor tie, was one of the kindest she had ever seen. Patty was making futile dabs at her soft hair. It was forever falling down, and her very clean petticoats were forever peeping below her skirt, and her shoelaces were forever trailing. Patty did not care. She lived for books . . . and for friends, and collected both in large numbers.

"It's *Martin Chuzzlewit*," she said in her breathless voice. "I'm trying to turn the book into a play and I want to ask you all whether this incident I've selected could be worked up for the second act."

Members of the Violent Study Club not only read aloud from books they liked; they used fellow members to test plot ideas, completed stories, and writing styles. The members took their responsibility as guinea pigs seriously, and the room became quiet at once.

"Please go on talking!" pleaded Patty. "I want to wait for Marbeth." Modest Marbeth Cliff was the most valued critic in the club.

"While we're waiting," said the President, "let's hear what the rest of you have brought."

Sigrid shouted, "Stephen Leacock! Funniest man alive!"

"A beautiful book called *The Song of the Lark,* by Willa Cather," said "Q."

"I know you all think Lowell is old-fashioned," Betsy said. "But I want to read, 'The snow had begun in the gloaming.' Because it *did* begin in the gloaming, and it's so lovely, and it's all over the trees and bushes, and goodness only knows how we're going to get home!"

"That's my wife!" said Joe. "I've brought Leonard Merrick's short stories. Grand technique!"

The magazine editor smiled meaningfully at the frail MacTavish. "We might hear a poem that one of our colleagues has just sold to my magazine. It's a war poem. A hum . . ." But the "dinger" was lost in a burst of unforced joy.

"The Naughty Chair! The Naughty Chair!" everyone cried at once . . . everyone except Tib who asked wildly, "*Was ist los?* Who's been naughty?"

No one answered. All the members were pulling the blushing MacTavish to his feet. They were pushing him toward a chair at one side of the fireplace—a tall, straight chair, carved of dark Indian mahogany with a yellow velvet seat.

Marbeth tried to explain. "We call it the Naughty Chair because Jimmy Junior has to sit there when he's naughty."

"But Jimmy Junior has gone to bed!"

"Yes, but when any member makes a sale he has to sit in the Naughty Chair."

"*Lieber Gott!* What's naughty about a sale?" Tib laughed until she almost choked. She swung her small feet off the floor to the sofa. "I'd better watch out. I'll be trampled to death in this *verruckt* club!"

MacTavish was pushed jubilantly into the place of honor. The President, beaming as though he had sold a poem himself, rapped noisily for order.

"You will all settle down—and sharpen your wits! I'm pleased that we have someone in the Naughty Chair tonight, for a most important visitor is coming—provided he's not stopped by Lowell's snowfall, or, more likely, ten beautiful girls."

"Jimmy!" Sigrid clapped. "Did you really get him?"

"I certainly did," President Cliff said proudly. "Rocky in person!"

Sigrid inspected her diamond. "Oh, if it weren't for this!" she murmured dreamily.

"He certainly is a charmer," smiled "Q."

"He's a genius," declared the serious man reporter.

"Ja, ja!" said Tib, in the soothing tone of one humoring infants. "Tell us about him, Mr. Cliff, please."

Jimmy settled back in his big chair.

"Rocky," he began, "is one of the last of a fast-vanishing breed, the tramp newspaperman. He never stays on any job long. But he's so good that every city editor welcomes him back. At twenty-seven he's been a star reporter in San Francisco, St. Louis, Kansas City, New Orleans, Minneapolis—some of you remember when he was here before."

Betsy looked inquiringly at Joe, but he shook his head. "While I was in the East," he said.

"He landed in town yesterday," Jimmy went on. "Brad put him on the payroll as soon as he walked in and the city room has been buzzing ever since. The men all stop work and listen when he talks; the girls all look when he walks by. He never went to college, but he's read everything. He came in yesterday with Ouspensky's *Tertium Organum* under his arm."

Tib threw up her hands. "Who's Ouspensky? What's Organum?"

"Joe's got a college degree," Jimmy said. "Ask him!"

"If I had a month free, I might try to answer." Joe grinned. But before he had time to make any attempt, firm, strong feet stamped themselves free of snow on the Cliff's front porch.

"Here he is, folks! The Great Rocky!" Jimmy said.

The young man whom Marbeth admitted was hatless. His hair was a tangled shock of rusty-brown curls and he combed them back with both hands, but they sprang up again with an electric vigor. He was only medium tall and would have seemed fat if he had not been so solidly muscled. His forehead was broad, his eyes were keen, and a firm chin was slashed by an enormous dimple. His lips were full, and the smile he turned on the roomful of young women and men was—yes, Betsy decided—sweet.

"Let's see!" said Jimmy. "You know all the newspaper folks . . . except Joe Willard."

Introductions began, and MacTavish rose from the Naughty Chair, but no one explained why he had been sitting there.

Rocky seemed to be casually measuring everyone in the room. He shook hands silently, smiling, and still smiling turned to the sofa, swung Tib's tiny feet to the floor, and settled himself alongside her, sitting cheerfully on his backbone.

"There aren't two smaller feet in the world," he drawled. "But they do take up a mite of room." And hauling out a worn bulldog pipe, he looked at Marbeth for permission.

Betsy looked at Tib, expecting the disdainful air, but Tib was regarding the newcomer with amused astonishment.

"Why do they call you just Rocky?" she asked. "Don't you have any other name?"

"I was Rocky in the cradle. I was Rocky when I took to my pipe at the age of four."

"*Four?*" cried Tib, round-eyed.

"The terrible Rocky is what folks usually say." He smiled at her, and after a moment Tib began to laugh. But the laughter gave way to an almost awed inspection.

Hooray! Betsy exulted inwardly. She and Tacy had failed with Mr. Bagshaw, but this looked very promising.

She turned to Joe, wanting to share her triumph. He, however, was looking at Rocky. And soon he and all the others were listening to Rocky, as well. They were listening willingly and with absorbed attention.

Patty did not read from *Martin Chuzzlewit*.

"No! No!" she whispered in an agony of shyness when Marbeth remembered to suggest it. Rocky discussed the Dickensian trace in G. K. Chesterton.

MacTavish's poem was mentioned, but it was not read. Rocky plunged into a discussion of the *Spoon River Anthology*. Willa Cather, strangely enough, sent him into a yarn about Jack London, whom he had known in San Francisco. He called the great London "Jack."

Rocky talked on and on, magnetically piloting the Violent Study Club into uncharted seas. Tib looked dazed when she jumped up at last to help Marbeth with coffee and doughnuts.

Talk became general, and someone referred to President Wilson's Preparedness tour. Colonel Roosevelt had long been urging preparedness, and now the President had fallen into line.

Rocky drew on his pipe. "I don't know what's got into the Professor," he drawled. He called the President, "Professor." "But I know one thing. We're going to be in this war if he doesn't keep his head."

Tib put down the coffee pot from which she was refilling cups.

"Don't you mean," she asked, "that we're going to be in it if the Kaiser doesn't stop sinking our ships?"

Rocky looked as surprised as though a canary had pecked him.

"See here!" he said. "What kind of talk is that from a girl named Muller?"

Tib's eyes darkened. "It's American talk," she answered, and Rocky's sweet smile broke across his face. He put his hand for a moment on her black velvet arm.

"Spoken like a pint-sized patriot!" he said.

Betsy waited anxiously. Tib smiled.

The Violent Study Club had never run to such a late hour before.

"My public will say I'm slipping if I try to be bright on this little sleep," said "Q," putting on her wraps. Marbeth flashed on the pillar porch lights, and everyone was exchanging good nights when Rocky came up to Tib. He looked at her with brightly quizzical eyes.

"Where can I find you?" he asked, and this time Betsy held her breath.

"Why do you want to know?" asked Tib.

"I'm going to take you to lunch."

And to Betsy's joyful amazement Tib named the store where she worked in the art department. She told him she lunched between one and two. She sounded almost docile.

The Willards, Tib, and "Q" left in the magazine editor's car, after pushing a cushion of snow from its top. Betsy could not bring up the subject most on her mind, but as soon as she and Joe were inside 7 Canoe Place, she burst out:

"Isn't it glorious? Did you notice how taken Rocky was with Tib? And she really liked him! Even after that spat about preparedness, she said she'd have lunch."

"Um-hum," murmured Joe, hanging up his coat and hat.

"I think they're very well suited," Betsy said. "You

195

know, Tib understands writers because of you and me."

"Um-hum," said Joe. He was halfway up the stairs.

Oh, dear! Betsy thought. Aren't men unsatisfactory! But it was too late to telephone Tacy, who would have shared her excitement. She followed Joe to their bedroom and kept on talking.

"I don't suppose he earns much, but you know Tib! Makes all her own clothes, and can get up a simply delicious meal out of nothing. Why, Tib was just meant to starve in a garret!"

Joe undressed and scrambled into bed. Betsy, in a pink cashmere robe, started to brush her hair. She brushed and brushed until it spread over her shoulders, dark and shining. Usually Joe liked to watch her do this but tonight he lay with his hands under his head, looking up at the ceiling.

Betsy began to worry. Maybe he wasn't just unsociable? Maybe he disapproved? She turned around, brush in hand.

"Darling," she said, "do you think I'm wrong? Don't you like this Rocky?"

Joe sat up in bed, and Betsy told herself that she must never allow him to wear any pajamas but blue ones.

"Look, Betsy!" he said. "Rocky's a good enough guy. But he lives in a different world from Tib's. He—has different ideas. He's—been around. I'm worried about Tib."

Betsy put down her brush, and sighed in relief.

"Is *that* all!" she said. "Well, you don't need to worry

about Tib! Men eat out of Tib's hand. He'll be following Tib around like a little puppy dog. Why—" Betsy began to giggle. "Tib will be tying a pink ribbon into that bushy hair of his."

"That," said Joe, "I'd like to see!"

But he chuckled, and went to sleep.

15
ROCKY

As soon as she woke up, Betsy telephoned Tacy.

"What shall we wear?" Tacy cried. "Yellow or blue?"

"Oh, the bride picks the bridesmaids' colors!"

"Well, it can't be pink, on account of my red hair!"

They were almost as jubilant when Betsy telephoned after the next meeting of the Violent Study Club. Tib had come with Rocky. She had left with Rocky.

"He calls her Tiny Tib."

"How cute!"

"She isn't haughty with him," Betsy said, a little puzzled. "She doesn't order him around."

"Maybe a masterful man is just what she needs?"

"I think you're right," Betsy replied.

But her enthusiasm began to wane. The Violent Study Club wasn't so much fun with Rocky there.

He dominated the once carefree meetings—sitting on his backbone, puffing at his pipe, being brilliant in his drawling voice. He had an engaging playfulness, sometimes, but it couldn't be trusted.

When others spoke, he listened with what seemed to be flattering attention, but then he tore their arguments to humiliating tatters. He discussed the books they brought with such scornful irony that no one felt free any more to bring just whatever he was enjoying.

"Irvin S. Cobb's *Speaking of Operations* is simply rich. But you have to bring Dreiser or Shaw to the club now," Sigrid grumbled.

As for reading their own work—the members were soon reluctant to expose themselves to his attacks, so unlike the friendly, helpful criticisms of pre-Rocky meetings. He followed his scathing remarks with an apologetic smile, but this no longer seemed charming. One night there was an indignation meeting in the kitchen.

"I wouldn't bring a story to the club any more for a farm."

"What magazines has he sold to? What books has he written? He's older than any of us!"

"Jimmy says he's a genius. But Jimmy finds excuses for everyone."

"Don't worry! We always break up in the spring, and he'll be gone before fall." "Q" 's words were consoling to everyone but Betsy. She was disturbed about Tib, who had sat looking at Rocky with an awe close to reverence.

Betsy understood. Tib's great capacity for admiration, in which she and Tacy had often sunned themselves, was called into full glow by Rocky's magnetism.

Betsy was as worried now as Joe, and Tacy started worrying harder than either of them.

"What do they have in common?" she asked anxiously. "Are they congenial? Do they like to do the same things?"

"I'll try to find out," Betsy said.

She made a date for lunch with Tib on a cold bright day and remarked casually over the restaurant table:

"Fine skating weather! You and Rocky doing a lot of skating?"

Tib laughed fondly. "Rocky's too fat for skating."

"Do you go dancing then?"

"Rocky thinks dancing is effete." Tib laughed again. "I asked him, as a favor, to come to the Radisson and watch Fred and me do a tango."

"Your tango is a poem."

"Rocky said he couldn't help believing that the human mind—any human mind—deserved a better problem than figuring how many steps to take and when to sway and glide."

Tib seemed to think this showed a superior intelligence and Betsy smothered her indignation.

"He doesn't like the theater, either," Tib volunteered. "He thinks it's silly for people to memorize somebody else's words and stand up in front of other people and spout them."

"What *does* he like to do?" Betsy asked.

After profound thought Tib said, "He likes to talk. And eat. We go a lot to that new restaurant—you know, where a chef in a white cap makes pancakes in the window? Rocky talks, and eats stacks of pancakes.

"That reminds me!" Tib added. "He likes *Sauerbraten* and you can't get it fit to eat anywhere, outside of a home. May I come out to your house some Sunday and fix *Sauerbraten* and ask him to dinner?"

"Of course, dear," said Betsy. "We'll ask the Kerrs and make it a party." She tried to sound enthusiastic but she was so perturbed that she went straight from the restaurant to the streetcar and out to see Tacy.

"She's feeling domestic about him!" Betsy groaned.

Tacy agreed that this was very bad. "But at least," she said, "the dinner will give us a chance to meet him. Harry is worried, too."

"He and Joe aren't joking us this time about being Little Aids to Cupid."

Tacy made coffee, and they cheered themselves with Kelly, who was shouting on the sun porch over a toy duck that was losing its stuffing.

"Won't it be nice," Tacy said, "for him to have a baby brother? Sister, I mean."

"I forgive you. What new words has he learned?"

"He learns some every day. And Betsy, he can understand even when we *spell*. Harry says, 'It's time for Kelly to go to b-e-d.' And Kelly shouts, 'Don' wanna b-e-d.'"

"That's the smartest thing I ever heard," Betsy said.

"Harry always makes a game of putting him to bed. After Kelly's undressed, Harry carries him around to look out the windows. He's made up a rhyme."

Tacy chanted:

> *We go around and turn out the light*
> *And we go to the windows and say good night*
> *To the moon and the stars that shine so bright*
> *And we go to bed, and everything's right.*

Kelly threw down his duck. He looked up at his mother with deep blue eyes, like hers.

"B-e-d!" he spelled. And Betsy and Tacy whooped with delight.

Betsy was pleased to have the joke to tell Joe. He was feeling a little blue these days. He didn't like it that his stories were still selling only to the same small magazines. He and Betsy tried each new story on the big magazines, especially on *The Thursday Magazine,* the biggest one of all. *The Thursday Magazine*, however, kept sending them back.

And the war news was grim. In France, big guns were thundering again. But the Germans, not the British, had launched the great offensive at Verdun.

And spring was slow in coming.

At first the snow which melted in the daytime froze at night. But at last water babbled in the gutters all night long. Watching for Joe, Betsy walked along Canoe Place to the corner. She waited among the sleeping houses, the dark apartment buildings.

" 'Behold the height of the stars, how high they are!' " she whispered sometimes, staring upward.

At last the glittering streetcar rattled into view, and Joe came swinging toward her.

If they talked long over their cocoa, they were interrupted by bird voices. While the world was still dark, there would be a drowsy chirp or two, then a small burst of song, then another, and finally a jumbled chorus. Joe and Betsy would go out on the porch. Blackness had now paled into gray, and the stars had faded—except for a big bright one in the faintly flushing East.

"Venus!" Joe would say. "In the spring, the morning star is Venus."

"It's the first time I ever watched spring come at night," Betsy observed.

Daytime spring was a more familiar joy, and yet there was a new ecstatic excitement in watching leaves bud on

203

their own lilacs, in poking around their own walls among matted leaves to see what was coming up.

"Iris and lilies of the valley," Aunt Ruth told them, examining the first green spears.

It was hard for Joe to get in any writing, but he almost always did, and when that was behind him . . . what raking and burning! What painting and digging!

Mr. Ray planted the cutting of that vine from Deep Valley. He and Joe planted hydrangea and bridal wreath bushes around the big porch.

Joe and Betsy bought their porch furniture. (He was head of the night copy desk now and had had another raise.) Just as planned, they bought a swing, wicker chairs and tables, and rattan curtains for when it rained. They started eating out.

"It's divine! We smell lilacs while we eat. Why don't you run over from school for lunch sometimes?" Betsy asked Margaret and Louisa, when they dropped in.

Louisa's eyes grew wide. "Oh, we couldn't, Betsy! He'd collapse! He'd die! He just lives for the noon hour."

Betsy thought, A clue at last! For Margaret and Louisa still alternated between Bill and Bub with mysterious unconcern. Betsy asked casually, "Who'd collapse? Bill or Bub?"

"Why, neither of *them*!" exclaimed Louisa. "I mean that Long-legs who works in the cafeteria."

Betsy was bewildered. She remembered vaguely hearing of such a boy, but a very long time ago.

Margaret interrupted with a sparkle in her long-lashed eyes. "Boogie! Don't be silly! I wouldn't even know his name if he didn't play basketball or something."

"Basketball or something! Betsy, he's a star! At everything long-legged. Basketball, track, tennis! You should see him at tennis. He jumps like a grasshopper when Bogie's at the matches."

"Even if she's with Bill or Bub?"

"All the higher then."

Margaret's slim foot put the swing into motion. She changed the subject with her Persian Princess air.

"You know, Betsy, that Julia and Paige are coming for their vacation. Well, what do you think Papa's going to do to celebrate? He's going to buy a car!"

"A car!" This news was so sensational that Margaret and Louisa had gone before Betsy remembered the long-legged tennis star.

Was *he* the reason Margaret had no choice between Bill and Bub? Margaret always kept her own counsel.

"And I didn't even get his name!" Betsy mourned.

In front of the house the maple trees were hung with lacy tassels. In the small back yard the apple tree seemed to be spreading arms to display its rosy bloom.

"Remember Mr. Aston?" Betsy asked Joe. "How he scolded me in high school English because I said apple blossoms were rosy? And you defended me."

"He was speaking to the future Mrs. Willard," Joe replied.

Sparrows settled in the birdhouse. This was intended for wrens, Aunt Ruth said, but sparrows were just as absorbing. The father perched on the roof, when he wasn't replacing the mother on four speckled eggs.

Sally Day came to see the spectacle. With a piece of Aunt Ruth's coffee cake, she sat on the kitchen steps announcing that she was going to sit there till the eggs hatched.

Brad Hawthorne dipped into a pocket for one of his little folded papers. "John Burroughs!" he said, and read aloud:

> *As the bird feathers her nest with down plucked*
> *from her own breast, so one's spirit must shed*
> *itself upon its environment before it can brood*
> *and be at all content.*

He looked at them keenly through his glasses. "You kids don't realize that yet, but it's true," he said.

Like Mr. Ray, he always called Joe and Betsy "kids"; Mrs. Hawthorne said lovingly, "you children." But they were Brad and Eleanor now to the Willards. Neither Joe nor Betsy was conscious of any difference in age between the Hawthornes and themselves—except when, as now, the Hawthornes shared their wisdom.

"Yes," Eleanor Hawthorne nodded. "You have to live in a house before it's home. Not just be happy in it, but work in it, suffer in it, build up memories."

"I'll remember Sally Day settling down with coffee cake to watch the sparrows hatch," said Joe.

"I'll remember Aunt Ruth telling me stories while the bread baked," Betsy said. She loved these nightly sessions, but in a few days she learned that they would end in the autumn.

She and Joe and Aunt Ruth were eating lunchbreakfast on the porch.

"I might as well tell you," Aunt Ruth said abruptly. "I've written my niece that I'll come to California in the fall."

"Why, Aunt Ruth!" Betsy cried.

"When did this happen, Auntie?"

"Oh," said Aunt Ruth, "we've been writing back and forth! Bertha says that together we can afford to buy a bungalow. And I can keep house while she teaches school. She's my own sister's daughter, and we've always gotten along. But I couldn't have gotten along with anyone better than I have with you and Betsy, Joe."

"You'd get along with anyone!" Betsy said.

"I have only one bone to pick," said Joe. "That homemade bread is making me fat."

Aunt Ruth wiped her eyes. "Well, I'm going to keep on making it till I leave. And I want to put up some things for you, Betsy. Strawberries, peaches, watermelon pickles, tomato preserves."

Betsy jumped up and kissed her. "We'll miss you, Aunt Ruth," she said, and knew she really meant it. "You've been so good to us!"

Aunt Ruth wiped her eyes again. "Well, I certainly

did appreciate you two taking me in! I was so upset about Alvin—and selling the store. But you know I've always wanted to go to California. I do hate the cold. I even tried to make Alvin move out there."

"We'll just have to have a good time till you leave," said Joe.

"We'll go riding in Papa's automobile!" Betsy jumped up. "Joe! I forgot! It's been delivered. It's out in front of 909 right now."

The new car was a fine black Overland and Mr. Ray displayed it proudly.

"What will Paige and Julia think of this, hey? It's got all the newest wrinkles. Get in, Joe! Take us for a ride!"

"Don't you want to drive, Dad?"

"I don't know how. And to tell you the truth," admitted Mr. Ray, "I don't want to learn. But Jule's going to learn. Aren't you, Jule?" he asked his wife coaxingly.

"I'm starting lessons tomorrow," she replied.

Joe took the wheel. Mr. and Mrs. Ray, Aunt Ruth, Margaret, and Betsy piled in and went whirling out into the country, past blooming orchards, brimming lakes, hillsides where wild plum was white.

"Oh, the picnics we'll have!" cried Mrs. Ray. And next day she did start driving lessons. But after two of them, she stopped.

"I got on better with Old Mag," she said. "Margaret's seventeen. Let Margaret drive."

So Margaret started lessons. But she didn't like driving, either.

"If you don't mind, Papa," she said politely but firmly, "I'm not going to do it."

Betsy wouldn't even try to learn. "I'm not the type," she shuddered. "I'd be making up a poem when I ought to be honking, or stopping, or something."

"I'm certainly glad you came into the family, Joe," chuckled Mr. Ray.

So with Joe at the wheel of an always overflowing car, they went riding almost every afternoon. There were snow drifts of bridal wreath now along Minneapolis streets. They called on Carney, and on Tacy, who always asked, "When is Tib going to cook that dinner?"

And at last Tib phoned to ask whether next Sunday would be a good day. She came out on Wednesday and put an enormous chunk of rump beef to soak in vinegar and water and bay leaf.

"It has to soak for four days," she said with delighted importance. "I'll be out early Sunday to set it stewing. I'm going to make potato dumplings, and we'll have new peas, and a little wilted lettuce."

"I could make an apple cake for dessert," said Aunt Ruth.

"*Wunderschön!* I'll serve it with whipped cream."

Betsy urged Tib to stay, but she couldn't. "I'm meeting Rocky for a movie. He doesn't like many movies, but he does like Charlie Chaplin."

"It doesn't matter to Rocky," grumbled Betsy later, "that *Tib* does like movies, and the theater, too." But as Sunday approached she cleaned and polished, wanting the house to be a credit to Tib. She picked iris for the vases, and Aunt Ruth's apple cake looked luscious but she would not let Joe cut so much as a sliver.

Tib came out straight from church, wearing a taffeta suit of Copenhagen blue, a tilted hat made from the same material, and a snowy feather boa. She divested herself of boa, hat, and jacket briskly and tied on a scrap of apron. She was excited and happy, chattering to Aunt Ruth, and while the beef simmered in a covered iron pot, she began to grate potatoes for the dumplings.

Betsy's heart softened toward Rocky a little.

Maybe he *is* the one for her, she thought, setting the table with fastidious care. You can't choose a husband for another woman. Maybe she likes him bossy and selfish. She certainly likes to cook for him.

He walked in shortly, in the spruce golfing knickers he liked to wear—although he scorned golf. Running his hands through his unruly hair, smiling his charming smile, he shouted, "Where's Tiny Tib?" He sniffed and tasted and Tib's laughter trilled.

Betsy's heart softened more and more.

The Kerrs arrived and joined the rest in the kitchen. Tib fluttered efficiently about. The tiny apron was quite inadequate even for her tiny person, but Tib never spilled or spattered. She was as dainty at cooking as at dancing.

They all sat down to the shining table.

"Some groceries!" Rocky kept saying. And he'd blow a kiss. "Here's to you, Tiny Tib!" Tib smiled with delight, and Tacy gave Betsy reassuring glances. He was nicer, she signaled, than she had expected him to be.

They lingered over apple cake, heaped with whipped cream, and second or third cups of coffee. Rocky was eloquent on a subject that was stirring the city. Mexican raiders under Villa had attacked a New Mexican town, and President Wilson had ordered Brigadier General John J. Pershing into old Mexico to catch the bandit. National Guard units had been called out—four regiments from Minnesota.

"It's almost the last straw for Hobbie," Tib said. "He's so wild to get into a uniform! I suppose it's being named for Hobson's-choice–Hobson that makes him so warlike." She repeated this family joke with her little tickled laugh, and the Kerrs and the Willards laughed too, but Rocky grimaced.

Rocky, Betsy remembered, was never very good humored when he wasn't doing the talking himself. Tib, too, seemed to remember and fell silent. But Tacy asked about Fred, and Tib brightened. He was graduating this month.

"With honors in architecture," she said proudly.

Rocky looked around as though appealing for sympathy. "I've heard of nothing but Brother Fred for a week now," he said. "Tib wants to drag me over to the Commencement exercises. As though no other male had ever got a sheepskin! Frankly, I'm a bit bored with the Muller family."

Betsy spoke quickly, resolved not to show her rising anger.

"The big news in the Ray family," she said brightly, "is the new automobile which no Ray will drive. Just Joe, who's only a Ray by marriage. Papa insisted on leaving it here tonight, on the chance we'd like a spin. Or we have some new records—'Nola.' 'Poor Butterfly.'"

"What would you like to do, Tib?" Joe asked, turning toward her with emphasized courtesy. Joe was angry, too.

Tib laughed a little nervously. She said what she almost always said in answer to such a question. "Oh, whatever the rest of you want to do!"

Rocky clapped his hands to the table.

"I wish, Tiny Tib," he said, "that just once you would express a preference. Do you really not like anything better than anything else? What shall we call her, folks? Miss Rubber Stamp? Miss Jelly Fish?"

Tib blushed to the roots of her yellow hair.

Betsy did not dare to speak. And neither Joe nor Harry—she could see by their furious faces—could be trusted either. She was thankful when Tacy took charge. The once shy Tacy had acquired poise since her marriage. Relief flooded into Tib's face as Tacy spoke with calm decisive graciousness.

"Let's drive around the lakes," she said. "I love to see

the street lamps making exclamation points in the water. Tib, that *Sauerbraten* was perfect."

She smiled. But alone with Betsy, when they went upstairs for wraps, her eyes flashed.

"I wish this tramp newspaper man would tramp on to Timbuctoo and leave our precious little Tib alone."

"The trouble is," said Betsy slowly, "I don't believe she wants him to. Oh, Tacy!"

16
"EVERYTHING'S ALMOST RIGHT"

One hot July day Joe did not write for just two hours as usual, but all afternoon. The study door did not open. The typewriter clacked on, and on, and on.

"We won't disturb him," Betsy said. "Not for anything." And she broke an engagement they had with the Rays. She and Aunt Ruth went softly around the house which was closed and darkened against the soaring heat.

"I wonder why he's writing so long," Aunt Ruth whispered.

"Oh," answered Betsy, "something just hit him!"

Pondering what it might be, she recalled a conversation early that morning. It had stayed hot all night and she and Joe had sat a long while on the porch where there was a little freshness. She had told him one of Aunt Ruth's stories of harvesting around Butternut Center.

"I remember that," Joe had said abruptly. "I was visiting there with Mother. It was before she died, and I was a very little boy. Someone let me take water to the men working in the fields."

"Maybe that set him off," Betsy thought.

She and Aunt Ruth were in the kitchen, preparing a cold supper, when they heard the study door open. Joe came downstairs looking fagged, and handed Betsy a sheaf of papers.

"Tell me what you think of this, will you?" he asked, and went outside, and began to water the lawn.

Betsy was making a salad, but she put it aside, washed her hands, and took the story up to her bedroom.

It *was* laid in the harvest fields. It was named, "Wheat."

When she finished reading it, she ran down to the yard. Joe dropped the hose and she threw her arms around him.

"I think it's perfectly wonderful!" she said.

"Any criticism?"

"No!" Her voice was puzzled. "It's rough. If it were my own, I'd polish it, probably."

"Then why shouldn't I?"

"Because it seems meant to be like that. It has a vigor, a power—you might polish that away. I think you'd better just copy it and send it off. Let me copy it for you."

"I wish you would," Joe said, "I don't want to look at it again."

That night after Aunt Ruth went to bed, Betsy typed the story in her best style, and the next day she and Joe mailed it to *The Thursday Magazine*.

Usually after they sent off a story, they discussed it endlessly. Would it sell? And for how much? And what would they do with the money? But about "Wheat" they did not say a word. It seemed to go off into a void. It was lost like a stone thrown in a lake.

Julia and Paige arrived, and the Willards were caught into a whirlwind. Julia always created an aura of excitement and gaiety. She was telling stories of the opera in New York, practicing for a summer opera engagement near Chicago, trying out people's voices. She scolded Tacy lovingly for neglecting her music.

"The more babies, the better you should sing. Look at Schumann-Heink!"

Julia played for everyone to sing.

There's a long long trail a-winding . . .

"Sing it in parts!" she commanded, and Bill and Bub

produced magnificent tenor and bass. Paige whipped out his flute and invented an obbligato.

He liked best to play his flute and go for automobile rides. Minnesota was so wonderful after New York, he kept exclaiming, although he and Julia loved New York; they wouldn't live anywhere else. Joe took them for countless rides. Wind rushed past their faces and they left the heat behind. There were thunder showers and ear-splitting crashes, and jagged arrows of lightning, and pouring rain.

"Sounds like the fourth movement of Beethoven's *Sixth Symphony*," Paige remarked.

After the rains, the leaves and roadways glistened. The birds sang and the wet lawns smelled of clover.

They took a picnic to Fort Snelling. Betsy loved the old army post—the round tower with its ancient musket slits, the commandant's house looking proudly down on the meeting of the waters. They went to Lake Harriet for band concerts and to Cedar Lake to swim.

Julia's skirts, Tib observed, came only to her shoe tops, and Tib turned up her own. She brought Rocky to meet Julia, who observed him closely for she knew all Betsy's qualms.

"He's wrong for Tib," Julia agreed. "I don't like it at all."

Julia wore her hair in deep soft waves—marcel waves, she said they were called. She took Betsy to a hairdresser for "a marcel." It was vastly becoming but the heat soon flattened it out.

"Never mind!" said Julia. "They're perfecting a machine that will put waves in *permanently*."

"Isn't science wonderful?" cried Betsy.

They talked war—and politics. The British had opened an offensive on the Somme. And in the United States a presidential contest was raging. It was Wilson against Hughes. Mr. Ray groaned at Wilson's campaign slogan, "He kept us out of war."

"He doesn't dare let them say, 'He'll *keep us* out of war.' He knows as well as Teddy does that war is coming."

"Papa! You must admit he's made the Germans restrict submarine warfare!" Julia had turned Democrat. Mr. Ray could hardly believe it. But the arguments were exhilarating, especially when Joe was around to bolster his father-in-law. Mr. Ray always hinted that Joe had inside information, straight from Colonel Teddy.

One Saturday afternoon Joe and Betsy stayed late at the Ray house, arguing.

"I won't have time to eat supper," Joe said, as they hurried home. "I'll just grab a sandwich."

Aunt Ruth was waiting on the porch.

"Any mail?" Joe called, as he always did.

"There's a letter for you," she answered, and he took the steps, two at a time.

The letter, lying on the old-fashioned table, was from *The Thursday Magazine*. "Wheat" was accepted. The editor hoped four hundred dollars would be satisfactory. He would like to see more of Mr. Willard's work.

Betsy flung herself into Joe's arms, crying and laughing. He was laughing, and almost crying, too. They caught Aunt Ruth into their hug.

"Oh, I'm so proud!" she cried.

"You helped!" Joe said. "Something you told Betsy about harvesting in Butternut Center started me off."

"Aren't you glad, Aunt Ruth," Betsy sang, "that we kept quiet while he was writing?"

"Oh, I'm so proud!" Aunt Ruth kept repeating. "Won't I have something to tell my niece, and her friends in California!"

Betsy rushed to phone the Rays. Their wild joy reverberated over the wire.

"Promise me you'll tell Brad," Betsy said when Joe had to leave, "and I'll phone Eleanor."

"All right," said Joe. "But don't tell the whole town."

So Betsy only telephoned Mrs. Hawthorne, who was rapturous, and the Cliffs, who cried out that they would dust the Naughty Chair at once, and the Kerrs, whose cheers woke Kelly, and Tib. Betsy did not expect to find Tib at her boardinghouse on a Saturday evening, but for a wonder she was!

"I'm so tickled!" she cried. "I'm coming right over. Could you put me up tonight?"

"Could we! On that couch in Joe's study. Aunt Ruth and I are simply bursting to talk."

Tib came as fast as the trolley would bring her, and Betsy showed her the wonderful letter and the check.

Aunt Ruth stirred up some cup cakes and they had a powwow over the evening tea. When Aunt Ruth went to bed, Betsy and Tib washed up the cups, chatting more quietly.

"Why aren't you with Rocky tonight?" Betsy asked.

"I wouldn't see him," Tib replied. She dropped her head forlornly on Betsy's shoulder.

"*Liebchen,*" she said, "you're lucky to have a husband like Joe."

"I know it," Betsy answered soberly. "He really loves me."

"*Ja,* and he *respects* you. He confides in you, listens to your opinions, asks your advice. He thinks your work is important. He thinks you are important—as a human being, not just as a girl."

Betsy hugged her, wanting to cry.

"Rocky and I," Tib said, "could never be partners like that. He loves me but he's always so contemptuous. He thinks I'm silly and prudish. Maybe I am prudish, but that's the way I intend to stay." After a moment she said, "I ought to go away."

"Tib, darling," Betsy began, but she was interrupted by a pounding on the porch door.

"Anyone home? Betsy—it's Rocky. Is Tiny Tib here?"

"*Ja,* I'm here," called Tib, and they went out to the shadowy porch, and Tib sat down in a corner of the swing as Betsy opened the door.

Rocky was coatless, and his hair stood on end.

"Whew!" he said, pushing it back. He stood looking down at Tib. "You led me a chase, little one! No message at your boardinghouse. I've been kicking my heels for hours."

"I told you I was busy tonight."

"I can't get along without you. You've gotten to be a habit. You're my opium."

Betsy started to go inside but Tib said, "Wait, Betsy! Please!"

"At least," Rocky said, "I can walk you home."

"I'm staying here all night," Tib replied.

"Then how about walking down to the lake a few minutes?"

"I'm sorry, no. But would you like me to make you some coffee?"

"No, thanks," he answered, almost gently. He sat down and stared at the floor.

"How about tomorrow?" he asked at last.

"Call me," said Tib.

"Couldn't I pick you up at church?"

"Just call me," Tib replied.

He went over and took her small face between his hands. "See you tomorrow," he said, and hurried out.

Tib was quiet in her dim corner. Betsy locked the porch door.

I wish I could lock him out of Tib's life! she thought.

She did not speak, and neither did Tib. Fireflies flickered under the shadowy maples. Down the street a phonograph was playing.

Tib stood up. "I'm going to call home," she said. "It's late, but Mamma won't mind."

They went inside and after Tib had given the Long Distance operator the number, she said in a shaky voice, "Mamma's worried about Hobbie. And Hobbie and I are good pals. I have quite a little influence with him. I think I'll be more useful there this summer than I would be in Minneapolis." She turned back to the phone. "Is that you, *liebes* Mamma?"

Betsy went out to the kitchen. She buried her head in her arms but she could hear Tib's voice. It sounded cheerful and natural. But when Betsy went back Tib was sitting in Joe's chair and tears were running down her cheeks. She didn't try to speak, but looked up at Betsy with a wordless appeal. Betsy hugged her closely and cried, too.

"Darling, if it's any comfort, I think you're doing the right thing."

"I know I am," Tib said in a small voice through her tears. "That's how I can do it."

She wiped her eyes, blew her nose, and spoke firmly. "I told Mamma I'd be down on the early train. So I won't stay here, after all. I'll go back now to my place and pack."

"I'll go with you," Betsy said. "I'll phone Joe to pick me up there."

"I'd like to have you."

"Well, you have me! You have both of us."

She had them, as a matter of fact, until her train left.

Joe waited on the boardinghouse porch until she was packed. And then it was too near morning to go to bed. They went to the depot, and drank coffee, and Joe joked, and Betsy hung on to Tib's hand.

Rocky went down to Deep Valley, Joe reported, on Monday. But he came back the same day.

"He seemed dazed. He couldn't believe any girl would turn down the Great Rocky. He resigned, and is off to Chicago."

Tib's letters did not mention this visit. Fred, she wrote, was going into their father's office; they'd be architects together. Her boss wanted her back. He didn't want to lose her. Nice, *nicht wahr?* But she was going to stay home until the start of Hobbie's senior year—and the football season. He was sure to be the quarterback. And he'd be all right then.

Julia and Paige were gone, and Aunt Ruth had bought her ticket, when Joe telephoned one August night to tell Betsy that he had some news. He wouldn't say what it was, but as soon as he stepped off the street-car, it came tumbling out.

"Brad is putting me back on the day side. To write. Features, mostly. He said I had what a feature writer needed—wit, a light style, an eye for the angles, and a gift for getting on with all sorts of people, from stage stars to truck drivers."

"Good!" exclaimed Betsy. "Every word true!"

"He said," Joe went on, "that he'd put me on the

night side last fall for two reasons. First, he'd had a hunch I could use more money, and that was the only spot in which he could give it to me. But second, because a young man who showed promise ought to be shifted around.

" 'But now,' he said, 'it's time for you to get back to writing. We can use a writer who sells to *The Thursday Magazine.*' "

"Joe! Joe! Joe!" Betsy cried, unable to express her prideful joy.

They sat on the porch swing, talking.

"Joe," said Betsy, "how beautifully this year has turned out! I was a little blue when you first went on night work, and Aunt Ruth was coming. But now—I almost hate to see her go."

"And I got the plot for 'Wheat' from her, in a way."

"And the night side gave us so much time for writing, and thinking, and talking. It certainly pays to wrestle with an angel."

"Let's get out the Bible and read the story of Jacob," Joe said.

"I'm going to do more than that," said Betsy with sudden vigor. "It's shabby the way I just go to church when I'm worried. I ought to go when I'm thankful and happy, too. I'm going to start going every Sunday."

"I've been thinking the same thing," said Joe.

Before that eventful August ended, Tacy's second boy was born. And after she returned from the hospital,

Betsy went out to the Kerr apartment. She went in the early evening, for Joe was still working at night. Tacy was in bed, the baby beside her, a brown-haired, brown-eyed elf.

"I just can't be sorry he isn't a girl," Tacy said.

"Neither can I. He's so sweet! And it *is* nice for Kelly to have a baby brother."

Tacy laughed. "That's funny," she said. "Before he came Harry and I talked about him always just in relation to Kelly. But now he's come, he isn't just Kelly's brother. He's himself. And we adore him."

"No wonder!" Betsy said, touching the soft cheek.

Harry was getting Kelly ready for bed. Splashes and shouts of laughter emerged from the bathroom, and at last, Kelly—curly-haired, flaming-cheeked, in snowy fresh pajamas, upright in his father's arms. They made the round of the windows and came to the bedroom. Kelly yanked down the shade, trying to join in his father's chant.

> *We go around and turn out the light*
> *And we go to the window and say good night*
> *To the moon and the stars that shine so bright*
> *And we go to bed, and everything's right.*

Harry held Kelly down to kiss his mother, and his brother, and Aunt Betsy.

"Everything's right!" When they were gone, Tacy put out a slim freckled hand, and took Betsy's, and squeezed it. "Everything *is* right; isn't it? Joe's story selling, the new job, and Harry and I with our new son. Of course it's not completely right," she added, "until things get right for little Tib."

"Everything's *almost* right," said Betsy.

Things couldn't be perfect, for herself or Tacy either, unless Tib was happy too.

17

JUST LIKE TIB

Tib seemed almost like Tib that winter, although Betsy and Tacy, who knew her so well, were aware that she was unhappy. Toward men who thought all blondes were frivolous she perfected a crushing disdain. With people who expected all German-Americans to be unpatriotic, she relied on the adage that actions speak louder than words. Her small skillful fingers made better bandages faster than any other ten in the Red Cross workroom. They were swift, too, on her drawing board, back at the store, and at making her own lovely fragile dresses. She had her accustomed good-natured cheerfulness.

She did not return to the Violent Study Club although that was its merry self again. Betsy knew it made Tib's heart ache to go to the places or do the things she associated with Rocky. She loved to go out to the Kerrs' and play with the babies, and she rejoiced wholeheartedly in the Willards' good fortune.

Joe had sold a second story to *The Thursday Magazine*. Betsy was able to save only a part of the magnificent checks. For their second wedding anniversary, he had bought her a wrist watch, and he insisted on buying her clothes—a blue, smartly belted coat and a furry blue felt hat. Bedecked with a chrysanthemum, she wore these to the Homecoming Football Game at the U. He bought her a swooping black velvet hat.

"It makes me look like a vamp," Betsy protested.

"Well, who vamped me?" Joe asked.

A coral silk dress trimmed with silver lace was fine for the nights they went with Sam and Carney to hear Dr. Oberhoffer conduct the Minneapolis Symphony Orchestra, and for plays at the Metropolitan. With Joe working days again, they were able to entertain. Betsy had learned a second company dinner. Chicken fricasseed in cream, and a marshmallow pudding!

She tried it out on Margaret and Louisa, who were charmed to be dinner guests. Margaret was soft-voiced and formal but Louisa exploded into excitement.

"This food is scrumptious!" she declared. "Isn't it, Bogie? And I heard you say, Betsy, that you didn't know how to cook when you got married. I suppose that after you get married you just sort of know how, automatically. Is that it? You're married, and so you're keeping house and so naturally you know how to cook. Is that the way it is?" And Louisa opened wide, inquiring eyes.

"Well, sort of!" Betsy said. "What's new at school?"

"A new drinking fountain!" Louisa cried. "No germs anymore! I don't know how we survived with that old cup on a chain. Really, I don't! But I'm certainly glad I did survive, because it's so nice to be a senior." She stopped. "You know, don't you, about the Senior Sleigh Ride? Bogie, have you told them?"

"How could I?" answered Margaret. "We only voted for it today."

"That's just it!" said Louisa. "It didn't take that Clay Dawson two minutes to get over to Margaret. Of course, he's got awfully long legs. That's why he's so good at jumping. He jumped over to her, absolutely jumped, and asked her for the sleigh ride."

"He's the boy from the cafeteria?" Betsy asked.

"That's right."

"Going with him, Margaret?"

"Oh, yes!" Margaret lifted pointedly indifferent

brows. "This pudding is delicious, Betsy. You ought to give the recipe to Anna."

"What," Joe could not resist inquiring, "are Bill and Bub going to do?"

"Both of them," replied Louisa, "are taking me! One on either side in the sleigh! Won't that be jolly? Oh, I hope we'll have lots of snow! Do you suppose we will, Joe?"

At Christmas time Anna fell ill of the grippe, and Betsy entertained the family. Joe stuffed the turkey and her mother brought the pies.

Christmas at 7 Canoe Place this year wasn't just a reflection of 909. The Ray traditions were all observed—stockings, joke presents, the readings, and the carols—but new Willard traditions were forming—the red Santa holding up mistletoe, window-candles to light the Christ Child on his way.

There was a doll under the Christmas tree. It was for Sally Day, who busily undressed it and draped it in a napkin to represent a fairy.

"I'm Queen of the Fairies, so naturally I have to have some fairies," she explained, rolling her eyes.

"I have an idea," Betsy said to Joe after everyone was gone, "that when Bettina comes, she'll be quite a bit like Sally Day."

"I think so, too," said Joe.

In one department, the Willards behaved parentally toward the senior Hawthornes, who always spent lavishly and then were rueful about their extravagances. On a mirthful New Year's Eve, budget-wise Joe and Betsy reckoned up what their prodigal elders should spend weekly, and what they might save.

"Why, we'll be millionaires!" Eleanor Hawthorne cried with mellow laughter.

"We can take a trip to Japan," Brad announced.

Joe and Betsy made personal resolutions. They were going to write and write and let nothing interfere. Betsy, in all her years of trying, had never made a sale comparable to Joe's sales to *The Thursday Magazine*. She didn't mind, but Joe did. He tried to put his finger on what was wrong.

"Your stories don't express you, Betsy. I think you need the meadowlike space of a novel. I'm going to make you start one in 1917."

But as February blew in, chill and bitter, 1917 began to reveal its own menacing purpose. The Germans resumed unrestricted submarine warfare, and President Wilson broke diplomatic relations with the Kaiser's government.

"It means war, Betsy," Joe said.

"Maybe not. Our troops are coming home from Mexico. That turned out all right."

She could not look war in the face, although she felt it staring at her. She treasured, more and more, the cozy, lamplit evenings at home.

"You were eating an apple and reading a book, the

first time I saw you," she reminded Joe one night, when he put down Charnwood's *Abraham Lincoln* to go to the kitchen for an apple.

The porch creaked and the doorbell rang. Joe turned back to answer it. Stamping snow from their feet on the threshold, were Tib and a tall young man.

"We've been skating," said Tib, which was obvious from her dress. She had long since made herself a skating suit, trimmed with white fur at the neck and around the closely-fitted jacket and the flaring skirt. The little peaked cap had a knob of fur. She was slapping her cold cheeks, laughing, and there was a look about her, Betsy thought quickly, that had not been there since. . . .

The tall young man had wavy dark hair, and bright dark eyes.

"Betsy and Joe Willard, Jack Dunhill! He's just back from Mexico," said Tib, as they came in, "and feeling gay."

"I'm feeling gay," he admitted, "but it has nothing to do with getting back from the Border. I just don't pick up a girl like this every day."

"It's a joke!" Tib explained. "He means he picked me up from the ice."

"That," said Joe, "I refuse to believe. Tib fall on the ice? Never!"

Tib and Jack Dunhill went off into gales of laughter.

"Well, she did tonight!" he said. "I was watching her perform, the conceited little monkey, and wondering who she was. Everyone was wondering and watching. I skated close, willing her to fall."

"And I fell!" trilled Tib. "And was I furious! Especially when he started picking me up, for he said he'd been watching me."

"And she said," Jack Dunhill put in, " 'I am *not* the blonde you've been looking for.' "

"And he said . . ." Tib bubbled with laughter, " 'How do you know you're not?' "

"The logical answer, wasn't it? And I suggested that we go somewhere for a cup of coffee and talk the whole thing over."

Tib sat down, pulling off the peaked cap. "And I said *Ja*, I'd go to have coffee, if he'd let me pick the place. And he said, of course he would. And so, here we are! He thought it was a restaurant until Joe opened the door." She laughed and laughed. "But we can have some coffee, can't we, Betsy, honey?"

"You certainly can," Betsy said. It was the first word either she or Joe had been able to get in since Joe's remark about Tib falling.

Joe took Jack Dunhill's leather jacket, and Tib ran upstairs. She came back with her curls pinned into place, and she and Betsy went to the kitchen.

Jack was an advertising man, Tib said as they made the coffee. "And you know, Betsy, I'm in advertising, in a way. I do art-advertising at the store. Jack wrote copy in a big advertising office. He went there right after he graduated from the U. And he gave up a good job when he left with the Guard for Mexico."

"It seems to me," said Betsy, "that you learned quite a lot about him, just walking up from the lake."

"Ach!" said Tib. "I walked him all around Robin Hood's barn, looking for that restaurant which didn't exist." And she and Betsy were still laughing when they wheeled a loaded tea wagon into the living room.

The men were briskly discussing the war.

"If we get into it," Jack was saying, "I'd like to be an aviator. Golly, how Pershing needed airplanes in Mexico! They could have sailed over those mountains where Villa was hiding, and we could have gotten somewhere. I've put in my application for aviation training."

"What's your rank in the Guard?"

"Lieutenant. I'm staying in for the time being."

"How do you like him?" Betsy asked Joe as soon as Tib and Jack were out of the door. "I like him," said Joe. "I like him a lot."

"I almost think it's the real thing."

"So do I."

"Do you? Oh, Joe, I'm so happy! I won't even tell Tacy. I'll just pray."

Tib phoned the third day. She was driving Jack's car. "It isn't a Rolls Royce but it's a perfectly beautiful Ford."

The next time, they had gone dancing. "He loves to dance. He's as good as my brother Fred. He's a marvelous skater, too, and he's going to teach me to play golf. I'll be good at it, he says."

And the time after that: "I wish Jack would hang on to his money. He has two thousand dollars in the bank. What do you think of that? But it won't last long with roses for me all the time and big boxes of candy. I'm taking him down to Deep Valley over Sunday."

Betsy broke down and told Tacy then. "I didn't call sooner for fear of jinxing it."

"I wondered," Tacy cried, "why she hasn't been coming out to see the baby! Well, phone me the minute she gets back! I can't bear this suspense."

"Neither can I."

"My folks are crazy about him," Tib reported on Monday. "He loaded Mamma with flowers. He and my dad talked golf, golf, golf, and he told Fred and Hobbie about the army. Hobbie brought half the boys in Deep Valley to meet him." Her tone grew serious. "Betsy, when can I see you and Tacy? I'd like to see you together. Can you come down to lunch with me soon?"

"We can!" Betsy cried. "Tomorrow!"

Tacy called for Betsy in the Buick around noon.

"Now don't get your hopes up!" Betsy warned, climbing into the auto. It was April weather, although the calendar still said March. The air was balmy, snow and ice were melting, and children were sailing boats along the gutters.

"Fine romantic day, though," Tacy said. "We could

almost have made it a picnic. I wonder why she wants us at the *Radisson*?"

"Don't wonder! Don't jinx it!"

"If you could know the trouble I had finding a woman to stay with the babies! But I'd have come if I'd had to bring them both."

Tib was waiting outside the swinging doors of the hotel.

"Come on in! Jack has reserved a table for us. He isn't rich like Mr. Bagshaw," she commented, "but he certainly knows how to do things."

He certainly did! The table bore three corsages of violets and roses.

"Tib, what *is* this?" Tacy asked, and Betsy's frown warned, Don't jinx it!

"I love a corsage!" she remarked in a careless tone.

As soon as they were seated, Tib stripped off her gloves. Brimming with smiles, she extended her hand to show a diamond.

"It's set in platinum," she said.

"Radisson or no Radisson!" Tacy cried and jumped up and kissed her. So did Betsy. Tib kissed and hugged them both.

"When did it happen?" Betsy asked.

"I guess it began when he picked me up off the ice. I never felt before the way I felt when I looked at him. He just—thrilled me. He still does."

"And when are you going to be married?" Tacy asked.

"That's what I want to talk with you about. Soon, because Jack thinks we're going to be in this war."

"That's what Harry thinks," said Tacy.

"Well, Harry probably won't have to go, on account of the children. But Jack will go. And I want him to, if he wants to. But of course we must be married first!"

"Of course!"

The waiter served their soup, but Tib did not touch it. She sat straight and spoke in a businesslike tone.

"I've been thinking," she said. "I don't want a hurried-up wedding. Both of you had that kind and mine ought to be different. I told Mamma so when we were talking it over. I told her I wanted a big beautiful wedding. She liked the idea.

"I want it to be in church, in our little St. John's Episcopal Church in Deep Valley. I want the church to be decorated with flowers, and I want everyone there, all the old Crowd.

"I want a white dress," Tib went on, shining faced. "I won't have a train. I'm too short. And do you know what else I want?" She looked up brightly.

"This is one reason I planned the big wedding. Did you ever stop to think that we'd never been bridesmaids for each other? It isn't right; we've been friends so many years. I'll have two or three more, of course. But I'm asking you two first. Will you be my bridesmaids?"

Would they! Betsy and Tacy braved the crowded dining room again to fall upon her with kisses. They pulled away to look at each other with laughing eyes. They said together:

"Isn't that just like Tib?"

"Why—why—what did I say?" cried Tib. "I just asked you to be my bridesmaids! There's nothing wrong with that, is there?"

"No, darling!" cried Betsy. "There's nothing wrong at all. Everything is beautifully, wonderfully, magically all right!"

18
THE NEST IS FEATHERED

"The world must be made safe for Democracy," said President Woodrow Wilson on the second day of April, and he asked the Congress to declare war on Germany. It did so. On April sixth he announced that a state of war existed.

"Betsy," said Joe, "you know without my saying so that I'm going to get in—and soon."

"I do know, darling!" Out in the purple spring twilight a robin's song went up and down, up and down.

A few days later he said, "There's talk of opening a camp for training officers. Out at Fort Snelling. I'd like that, if I can make the grade."

"It would be wonderful. You wouldn't be going too far away for a while."

The Officers' Training Camp was soon officially announced. It would open early in May and would commission successful students after three months of study. Jokes came thick and fast about Ninety-day Wonders.

"What if West Point does take four years to make a lieutenant!" Betsy cried indignantly. "We haven't got four years."

"If only I'm accepted," Joe grinned, "they can call me anything." With hordes of other young men, he submitted a summary of his college and employment record and the three required letters of recommendation.

"Imagine!" Betsy cried to her mother. "He's been back less than three years but a Federal Court judge and a big banker wrote two of his recommendations." His managing editor had written the third.

"Even those good letters," Joe said, "may not be enough. The camp can take only twenty-five hundred men. Lots more than that are applying. Sons of millionaires! Fellows backed by United States senators! Football stars! The competition is something fierce."

"You'll be accepted," Betsy said.

It wouldn't do any good if he wasn't, she thought. He'd just enlist and be gone all the sooner.

Betsy did not feel very patriotic, although she tried to. Patriotism had burst out all over, faster than spring. Flags like tricolored trees rose above factories, offices, and homes. Flags like tiny flowers bloomed in buttonholes. Tib wore one when she left for Deep Valley to get ready for her wedding. Carney and Betsy wore them when they went down to Nicollet Avenue to watch the Loyalty Parade.

Sam had applied for Officers' Training, too.

"He's warning me," said Carney, "that if he gets out from under my thumb he's going to grow a mustache and *wax* it."

"Joe," said Betsy, "will probably grow a beard."

The parade rang with martial music, as sunshine glittered on horns and trumpets, tubas, clarinets, and the jubilant sliding trombones. Drums beat and a field artillery regiment was shouting:

> *Over hill, over dale,*
> *As we hit the dusty trail,*
> *Oh, the caissons go rolling along. . . .*

You heard "The Star Spangled Banner" at the movies, at the theater, wherever you went. Up and down Canoe Place phonographs were spinning out "Tipperary," "There's a Long, Long Trail," and "Keep the Home Fire Burning."

"I don't want you to keep the home fires burning

here," Joe told Betsy. "I don't want you to be alone."

"I'll go back to 909," said Betsy. "The folks are urging me to."

"I'd want you to pay board."

"Yes, of course."

"Let's get this place rented then," he said.

"Furnished!" said Betsy firmly, and they put an advertisement into the *Courier*. The cottage was snapped up in no time. The renters had a little girl. She would like it, Betsy thought, that wrens were nesting in the bird house.

Betsy went briskly about the business of packing away dishes and silver and the most precious wedding gifts. She took down the box that held her wedding dress, and opened it, and put her face into the soft white silk. But tears came and she put the cover on again for she was sternly resolved not to cry. She added the box to the pile they would be taking to 909.

They made the last trip on a warm soft Sunday. Neighbors were uncovering flower beds, raking and burning, and birds were scouting through the budding trees. The shrubs had greened over. The bridal wreath Mr. Ray and Joe had planted would soon be in bloom. Betsy tried not to think about it.

If it takes something more than joy, and love, and happy memories to feather a nest, this one's feathered, she thought, but she acted busy and cheerful. She did not want to weaken her courage—or Joe's.

Not that there was much danger of weakening Joe's. Exhilaration was mixed with his sadness at renting the house and leaving Betsy, although he worried about her and she knew it. Shifting a dozen parcels, he found her arm and squeezed it as they walked away.

They settled themselves in Betsy's old blue and white bedroom, with their favorite books and other dear belongings—the long-legged bird, Joe's mother's vase, and the Goethe cup—in spite of the fact that it came from Germany and Joe would be fighting the Germans. The curtains had been freshly washed, and there was a big bouquet of daffodils. The whole house was flower-filled in welcome.

We're awfully lucky, Betsy reminded herself as they fell into the pleasant home routine. Joe was still working at the *Courier*, and watching for the postcard which would tell him he had been accepted at the Officers' Training Camp.

Coconut cake, Mr. Ray complained, was coming out of his ears, and Anna switched to strawberry shortcake. Mrs. Ray mentioned the government's request for meatless and wheatless days.

"Meatless and *wheatless*, Anna," she emphasized.

Anna snorted. "Meatless, yes, if the President says so. But he's eating well in the White House. Joe, poor lovey, is going off to fight the Kaiser." (Single-handed, she implied.) "And Joe was always one for dessert." She whisked a batch of cookies into the oven.

Mrs. Ray was almost as indulgent. She was being careful, Betsy could see, not to express unnerving sympathy, but her every word and glance was tender. Mr. Ray, like Joe, was excited about the war. He thought the United States had done right in entering. But his eyes were anxious when he looked at Betsy.

Margaret was the easiest one to be with. Shyly delighted to have her sister at home, she came to Betsy's room or followed her about, sometimes with Louisa.

"Betsy," said Louisa breathlessly, "tell me something important! When Joe is through at Fort Snelling, and an officer, will soldiers salute him?"

"I suppose so."

"And will he salute back?"

"Why, yes!"

Louisa heaved an enormous sigh. "Then when Bill and Bub are officers, *they'll* be saluted. I'll certainly feel proud."

"Are Bill and Bub going after commissions?" Betsy asked.

"They'll be training at the U next fall."

All the high school seniors who wanted to enlist were being given their diplomas, Margaret said, and one day she came home with a luminous face. Clay had enlisted! With all the Commencement glories right around the corner! He had come to school in his uniform, she said.

Next day he came to the Ray house, tall, gangling,

and sheepish in olive drab. Margaret made lemonade for him. She brought out cookies. She walked with him proudly up and down the block and introduced him to the neighbors.

"How do you like Clay?" she asked Betsy.

"Oh, I like him!"

"I'm wearing his class pin," said Margaret. "Nothing serious. I'm just sort of taking care of it while he's over there fighting. He's going to send me a silk handkerchief from Paris, and some German shells and things."

One Friday morning when Margaret was in school, and Mrs. Ray had gone shopping and Betsy was alone in the house except for Anna who was making a rhubarb pie, the mail brought the postcard Joe had been waiting for. He was to report at Fort Snelling the following Monday.

Betsy went straight to the telephone. He was excited, overjoyed, triumphant.

"I made it!" he cried. "By Gosh, I made it! I was more worried than I let you know, honey. Sam's in; he just called me. What day do I report, do you say?"

"Monday."

"Then I'll tell Brad and clear out my desk. Golly, I'm relieved!" He checked his enthusiasm. "You all right, dear?"

"Oh yes, sweetheart!"

"You know I'll be practically at home all summer."

"You bet I do. I'm going downtown right now and

buy some pretty summer dresses, and a big floppy hat with flowers on it to wear when I come to the Fort."

"Planning to vamp me, eh?"

Betsy went slowly upstairs. She put on her suit and hat and threw a fur around her neck. She tucked the little flag into her buttonhole and went out of 909 where a bigger flag was waving in a sweet May morning. Mr. Ray had the biggest flag in the block.

Joe had said he would clear out his desk. He would come home tonight bringing his dictionary, and the tennis shoes and racquet he always kept in his locker for tennis with Sam after work. Sam would be doing the same sort of housecleaning.

Like Grandpa Warrington, Betsy thought, coming across the cornfield with his school books and the big bell sitting on top! *"And the minute Grandma saw it she began to cry."*

War! Betsy thought, holding back her own tears with all the force of her stubborn will. War! Women never invented it.

She did not buy any new dresses, nor the big floppy hat, but went straight to the Marsh Arcade, and up the stairs to the second floor and the Hawthorne Publicity Bureau.

This was the happy office of which Joe had told her so often. One of the girls whose romances Mrs. Hawthorne had watched with such interest sat behind a desk. Mrs. Hawthorne's reddish-brown head was bent over another typewriter. At the sound of the opening door, she looked up with her queenly air but, seeing Betsy, she rose quickly, affectionate concern flowing into her face.

"Joe's card has come. He goes to the Fort Monday."

"That's hard."

Betsy nodded.

Mrs. Hawthorne kissed her, but she turned quickly and brightly. "I want you to meet my secretary, Celia. She knows Joe."

The small merry-faced girl smiled without speaking. Betsy smiled and sat down.

"Eleanor, I came for advice. I want to work while Joe's gone, but I want to do something that's helping in the war."

Mrs. Hawthorne's low laugh rang in welcome. "Just hang up your hat!"

"You mean . . . ?"

"We're up to our ears in war work; aren't we, Celia? Half our clients are launching campaigns. Recreational centers at army camps, for example. There's a big project for such a social center at Fort Snelling. How would you like to be sent out there for some assignments during the summer?"

"Oh, Eleanor!" Betsy winked away tears. Mrs. Hawthorne ignored them.

"When do you want to start?"

"Next Monday. The same day Joe does."

"Be here early! We need you desperately. And about salary?"

"Can we talk that over Monday?" Betsy murmured, and fled.

That was a stirring weekend at the Rays'. Everyone was pleased about Betsy's job. And Joe brought home not only the dictionary, the tennis shoes and racquet, but a poem Jimmy Cliff had written about the boys from the office who were going into the service. There was a verse about Joe:

> *No matter what happens to Willard*
> *Where demons of Shrecklichkeit stalk*
> *There'll still be a trace of a swagger*
> *A don't-give-a-damn in his walk. . . .*

"I never knew how to describe your walk before!" Betsy cried, and Joe winked at her.

"That's just Jimmy talking!"

On Saturday Mr. Ray brought home a service flag, with a big red star for Joe.

"We won't hang it until Monday," he announced with great conservatism.

"We'll soon have to exchange it for a flag with two stars," Mrs. Ray said. Paige was going in too, Julia had written.

Sunday night lunch was crowded with guests, come to say good-bye to Joe.

"Going all the way to the Mississippi River. Must be five miles," he joked to Tacy and Harry.

Sam was picking him up at five the next morning.

They wanted to be at the Fort by daybreak. So the party broke up early, and Joe and Betsy went to their room.

Joe began to put things into the one small bag he was taking, talking about the next day. He'd present the postcard, he planned, and then he'd be given a physical examination, probably, and be assigned to a company, a squad, his barracks, and pick up his olive drab.

"I'll send my civies back here. Then we'll be given rifles and start drilling."

"And Saturday noon you'll come home."

"I'll come on the double. And we'll go dancing. Or canoeing on Lake Harriet, maybe."

"And I'll be coming to the Fort, on assignments. Wearing that big new hat I'm going to get."

"And I'll say to the fellows, 'That's my girl.'" He broke off. "Where's your picture, Betsy? The one you had taken in your new coral silk dress?"

She found it for him.

"Write on it," he said. And she wrote across it, "Betsy."

Joe took the pen and added, "who is the loveliest lady in the world."

All of a sudden, in spite of herself, Betsy began to cry.

Joe took her into his arms. "Honey, honey, don't do that! Just when we're making such nice plans!"

"But the summer . . . won't last forever. You . . . you'll be going overseas."

Joe's arms tightened. "Listen, Betsy! Listen hard! I'm

coming back. Do you hear? I'm coming back. And I'll love you even more than I do now, if that could possibly be. I'll miss you so."

Betsy wept softly.

"Nothing in the whole world could come between you and me, Betsy. We're . . . woven together. You know that. And darling, when I come back we'll have our little home again. We'll have Bettina."

"How do you know all these things?" Betsy asked through her tears.

"I know," he said. "I feel it in my bones." And he held her closer and let her cry as long as she felt like crying.

19
BRIDESMAIDS AT LAST

When the bridesmaids arrived at the small, stone, ivy-covered church, organ music floated out to meet them. They hurried up the steps—fanciful figures in lilac and yellow organdy with large organdy hats—drawing "Ohs!" and "Ahs!" from neighborhood children crowded along the canopy. Tacy's eyes sparkled toward Betsy.

"At last!" she said.

"At last!"

Tib had designed their costumes. Tacy, Carney, Alice, and Winona wore yellow with lilac sashes and hats. Betsy, as matron-of-honor, wore lilac with a yellow sash and hat. In the vestibule they were given flags to carry.

"What a grand idea it was," Tacy whispered, "to make it a military wedding!" Betsy nodded and they tip-toed to peek into the nave.

Flags along the wall melted into the ruddy hues of the stained glass windows. Candles beamed on the altar. Roses and delphinium made a garden of the chancel, and bouquets were tied to the front pews.

The church was almost filled, although the grooms-men, trim and erect in newly tailored uniforms, were still seating a few late comers. Looking around the church, Betsy thought, was like taking a long happy look back over her own life, and Tacy's—as well as Tib's.

Her eyes picked out Tib's Aunt Dolly from Milwau-kee, whose beauty had so enchanted them as children when she came to visit in Tib's chocolate-colored house. The hotel owner's actress-wife who had taught Tib to dance. Their curly-haired algebra teacher, and almost all the old high-school Crowd. Tacy's sister Katie and her husband, come from Duluth. All three Rays.

A groomsman, one of Jack's brother officers, was es-corting Jack's mother to a pew on the right side, and whispers in the vestibule caused Betsy and Tacy to turn.

"Is it time to take Mrs. Muller down?"

"No one can be seated after the bride's mother, you know."

"Well, Tib's getting out of the car!"

Another officer groomsman gave his arm to Mrs. Muller. Short, plump, and calm in a gray, crystal-trimmed dress and turban, diamonds in her ears, she was escorted to the pew of the bride's family, on the left.

And back in the vestibule, Tib came in, a snowy cloud on the arm of her father who was almost bursting out of his cutaway with solemn emotion. Smiling, serene, she revolved for the bridesmaids. Her dress was made of chiffon, in bouffant style. The point-lace veil which framed her flowerlike face and cascaded all around her had been Aunt Dolly's wedding veil.

"Aunt Dolly never looked lovelier," Betsy thought.

The wedding party lined up for the procession and whispers died into silence. The brooding organ music ceased, and the church was charged with electric excitement by the strains of the wedding march.

The rector in his sober robes came out of the vestry room, followed by Jack Dunhill and Tib's tall, fair brother Fred, both in uniform. They walked out to the chancel and stood waiting.

With a click of heels the groomsmen came down the aisle. They walked two and two. Jack's brother officers first, then Joe and Sam, sternly military of stride and bearing, determined that Ninety-day Wonders, in training, should acquit themselves no less well than National Guardsmen, even though the latter wore officers' bars and sabers. Sam's waxed mustaches ended in gleaming needles.

Behind them, slowly, to the music's stately beat, came the bridesmaids. Tacy and Carney, followed by Alice and Winona, and then Betsy, alone—trying to remember to stand straight and not to smile. They might smile to Mendelssohn, coming back, they had been told at rehearsal.

Now it was Wagner:

Here comes the bride,
Here comes the bride . . . .

Betsy could not see the bride, just eight beats behind, but all along the aisle she heard breath caught in delight, and she saw the look in Jack's dark eyes as he stepped forward.

The groomsmen had divided and taken their places; the bridesmaids divided, and Betsy stationed herself on the left opposite Fred. She was worrying about receiving Tib's bouquet. Fred, no doubt, had the ring on his mind.

Tib arrived. Her father gave "this Woman to be married to this Man," and joined his wife. Jack and Tib, with Fred and Betsy, moved up toward the altar and Betsy took the bouquet without mishap, and Fred produced the ring.

The vows were echoes in Betsy's ears of the vows she and Joe had taken:

> *. . . for better, for worse, for richer, for poorer,*
> *in sickness and in health, to love and to cherish*
> *till death us do part. . . .*

The ring went on Tib's finger; she received her bouquet safely; Jack kissed her and they turned radiant faces as the Mendelssohn Wedding March sounded its great peal of joy.

At the chancel steps, they paused. Tib waited with complete composure, smiling. One of the two brother officers spoke in a low voice, and, as the wedding guests gasped, two sabers flashed out and clanged together to make an arch. When Jack and Tib, laughing, had passed through, the sabers flashed back into their scabbards again.

Each groomsman joined a bridesmaid for a gay race up the aisle and out to the vestibule where now a second garden bloomed. As soon as she had kissed Tib and Jack, Betsy ran to Joe. He looked so wonderful in his olive drab, she thought! He was tanned from drilling in the sun, and above his brown cheeks his hair looked almost silvery.

The Fort Snelling contingent had arrived just a few hours earlier, for they had only a two-day leave. Betsy, Tacy, and Carney had come to Deep Valley the day before, and Betsy had many gaieties to describe as the Rays and the Willards drove to the Muller house through the late afternoon sunshine.

Jean had given a shower for Tib. It was strictly for

ladies, but Cab had attended, beaming, in a uniform.

"Spickest, spannest private in the U.S. Army!" Jean had declared, patting his arm.

"Jean's going back to North Dakota to stay with her parents," Betsy reported. "And she says the baby will come before Cab gets back, if the Kaiser doesn't hurry and give in."

Betsy and Tacy had stayed with Cab and Jean, for the Muller house was overflowing with relatives.

"And this morning," Betsy said, "Tacy and I went off by ourselves. We went up to Hill Street and saw where we used to live."

Hand in hand, they had stared at the two houses, now so surprisingly small, which faced each other at the foot of the green billowy hills. They had drunk at Tacy's old pump. At the cottage which once had belonged to the Rays, they had looked up fondly into the back-yard maple, where Betsy used to write her stories and keep them in a cigar box.

Hand in hand, they had climbed the Big Hill which rose behind Betsy's old house. How many times they had climbed it—with Tib along, of course—taking picnics or exploring or just picking flowers! Today they had picked wild roses, pink and very fragrant, which were growing everywhere.

Reaching the top, they had sat down in the grass, just as they always used to do, to survey the town in its broad valley. They had particularly liked to look down on their own rooftops and the tower of Tib's chocolate-colored house.

"We thought that was the most wonderful house in the whole wide world," said Tacy.

"Because it had front and back stairs, and a tower room, and colored glass in the front door."

Joe was stopping the Overland in front of it now. As the Rays and the Willards went up the walk they saw a service flag in the tower-room window. It bore two stars, one for Fred and one for Hobbie who dashed up to take charge of Margaret.

If Cab was the army's spickest and spannest soldier, Hobbie was its proudest recruit. He somehow managed, although he was short, with embarrassing dimples, and a uniform which fitted nowhere, to look hard and military.

"The day that boy lands in France," said Joe, "the Kaiser had better start ducking."

The door with the ruby glass in it was open, and again music sang a welcome. A three-piece orchestra was playing in the hall where Mr. Muller, stout and jovial, and tranquil Mrs. Muller, greeted them.

Betsy hurried her parents and Joe into the study to see the wedding presents. Jack had given Tib an electric sewing machine.

"It was all she wanted," Betsy said. "And she's just ecstatic about it."

The study glittered with china and crystal, silver bowls and platters, embroidered linens from relatives of

Jack in England. But Betsy was called away to join the receiving line in the flower-filled, round, front parlor.

Tib's hand was tucked into the crook of Jack's olive drab arm. Tall and straight, he smiled down at her and she smiled back, when she wasn't being kissed. Beneath the point-lace veil and her golden cloud of hair she was rosy from being kissed.

The bridesmaids were busy greeting the visiting relatives. Betsy was pleased to see Tib's Milwaukee relatives again. Grosspapa and Grossmama Hornik, uncles, aunts, and cousins. Aunt Dolly was fortyish now, but still very fair.

There were old friends to talk with, too. Dennie, engaged to Winona. The siren Irma and her young doctor husband. Katie and Leo, who were teasing Sam about the mustache.

"Doesn't he look elegant?" Carney crowed. "But I have to be darned careful when I kiss him, not to stab myself."

At supper, most of the old Crowd squeezed in at the Bride's table. There were plenty of tables—in the spacious back parlor and all around the porch, which had a view of the sunset. Waiters hurried hospitably everywhere with cold turkey and ham and potato salad and hot, scalloped dishes and fresh rolls and pickled herring and anchovies and olives. But at the Bride's table, when it was time for toasts to be offered, Jack's brother officers jumped to their feet.

"Draw, SABER!" And the sabers flashed and crossed above Tib's head while Fred gave an Army toast to the bride.

"Do it again!" she cried, with happy laughter, and they did.

Using Jack's sword, and with Jack's strong hand guiding hers, Tib cut the wedding cake. There were favors inside!

Dancing began in the parlors and out on the porch, where the sunset had faded now. The evening sky looked like the inside of a shell. Jack and Tib led off, and then Tib turned to her father while Jack sought smiling Mrs. Muller. Soon everyone was dancing. Mr. and Mrs. Ray danced, he like a stately ambassador, she like a leaf in a breeze.

The older guests began to go home, except for the Muller relatives who gathered in the dining room. They were laughing and talking with Tib's father and mother over steins of beer. Betsy and Joe, dancing past, paused to look in.

The speech in the dining room was German because Grosspapa and Grossmama could not understand English very well. But in that enemy tongue. . . .

"To the Herr Doktor Wilson!" cried Grosspapa Hornik, raising a foaming mug.

"*Und* Teddy!" put in Grossmama.

"*Ja*, to the Herr Teddy!"

"Teddy!" and the steins banged.

"It does something to my heart," Betsy whispered to Joe who answered soberly, "What a wonderful country we have!"

They started dancing again. Jack was dancing only with Tib now, and Joe only with Betsy, and Harry with Tacy, and Sam with Carney, and Cab with Jean, and so on down the line. They sang as they danced. "Poor Butterfly!" "Pretty Baby." "The Sunshine of Your Smile!"

> K-K-K-Katie
> Beautiful Katie

How Hobbie—that hard, dimpled, military man— roared to that one, swinging Margaret!

They sang and danced to the war tunes—to "Tipperary," and "Pack up Your Troubles," and "Good Morning, Mr. Zip, Zip, Zip!" They were dancing to "The Long Long Trail" when Joe danced Betsy out to the porch, into the starlight and the warm June darkness, scented with honeysuckle.

> There's a long long trail a-winding
> Into the land of my dreams. . . .

She was in the land of dreams now, Betsy thought. The future and the past seemed to melt together.

She could feel the Big Hill looking down as the Crowd danced at Tib's wedding in the chocolate-colored house.

High School Hijinks!

*Join the fun with Betsy, Tacy, and the Deep Valley Crowd
in these other books in the Betsy-Tacy series:*

Heaven to Betsy

Betsy and Tacy are growing up! It's Betsy's freshman year, complete with studies aplenty and parties galore. Her dearest friends are all there, and some exciting new ones, too—including boys! Betsy's quite certain she's found heaven at Deep Valley High.

Betsy in Spite of Herself

Betsy Ray is now a sophomore, and she and her crowd are in the thick of things at Deep Valley High. Between studies and socials, the new Miss *Betsye* Ray is busy juggling her duties as class secretary. But the old Betsy isn't too busy to notice the oh-so-cosmopolitan stranger who has suddenly appeared on the scene. . . .

Betsy Was a Junior

Betsy's junior year promises to be a golden one, especially since one of her best friends from childhood, Tib Muller, has moved back to Deep Valley. Betsy is even inspired to start up a sorority at Deep Valley High—but the consequences are far more disastrous than she dreamed.

Betsy and Joe

Betsy's always had a crush on handsome, elusive, intriguing Joe Willard. And now, in her last year at Deep Valley High, she's determined to go with him. Of course, it's not as easy as it sounds—but when a girl is as determined as Betsy, anything is possible!

**Read all the books in the Betsy~Tacy series,
now available from HarperTrophy:**

Betsy~Tacy

Betsy~Tacy and Tib

Betsy and Tacy Go Over the Big Hill

Betsy and Tacy Go Downtown

Heaven to Betsy

Betsy in Spite of Herself

Betsy Was a Junior

Betsy and Joe

Betsy and the Great World

Betsy's Wedding